Druck und Distribution im Auftrag der Autorin:

tredition GmbH, Heinz-Beusen-Stieg 5, 22926 Ahrensburg, Deutschland

A first beat

L.H. Kuhrau

Preface

Thank you for choosing to read the last book in the "A first..." series. You will become a part of the main characters story, while you will step by step will see him grow. Each chapter defines one year, while you in the end will come into the presence, is the rest of the book written in past tense out of the main characters perspective.

Please be aware that the following book contains violence, torture, mental illnesses, loss, critical educations and other contents that might be sensitive to some readers. For further information, please check out the book subscription.

Enjoy the reading!

A first **Beat**

A first **Death**

A first **Suffer-ring**

A first **Mistake**

Welcome

My entire body was covered with blood. A final scream continued to reverberate through the air, only to be replaced by a continuous beep. Everyone was in a rush, sprinting both forward and backward. Nobody would give me any attention or check if I was alright. I remained a mere prop in the drama, on the sidelines, as the blood began to pierce my heart. It gradually became one of the most recognizable aromas, flavours, and harmonies I would ever encounter. Even someone who took up a mobile phone would just take a call or picture. Perhaps my memory wasn't in the best of shape. I remained silent, looking at the event in front of me; nobody would even notice that I was there at all. As long as the primary issue was being addressed, no one seemed to care. That's how the first beat of my heart became the first kill at once, while I learned that nobody would ever care. If they didn't receive compensation for caring for me, they would simply perform their duties; regrettably, they were unable to do so on that particular day. Ava

Farell Farris, who gave birth to me, died at 1:15 am, precisely at the age of 21. What a wonderful birthday gift I had given her!

The other day, at 3 a.m., my father discovered the truth. There was nothing he could have done. Afterwards, I occasionally questioned whether they desired her death. She was a strong woman, as my father would always say. She was too stubborn for the world she would be thrust into, despite my father's constant attempts to save her. To imagine them, while having heard his stories, was just disgusting. Love. Nothing mattered in our world, and therefore I would get away from him as fast as possible. Additionally, it worked to my advantage that his boss, not him, was raising me.

My father, Sandey Farell Farris, is the one who works closest to the world's most powerful man. Others might refer to him as a henchman, and while there were numerous advantages to this role, I always maintained a strong sense of friendship between us. Neither is a good thing to have. You should not hold onto any emotions or relationships that you fear losing. Once you have them, they will be what you desperately have to protect, since they are in the middle of the shooting target for all your enemies. On my first day, I would have more than enough from there.

Conversely, I didn't exhibit much patience either. As soon as someone picked me up, my first instinct was to bite him in the fingers. It wasn't just anybody. No. He was my father's boss, a person you definitely don't want to get into a fight with. At the time, he was 56 years old and had personally caused at least ten times as many deaths. Still, I am alive. At the age of seventeen, I am writing this. There must have been something that briefly sparked his heartbeat. Not that my bite was any harmful, but he had killed people just because they looked at him before. He wasn't charming, friendly, or in need of being polite, either. From his first day on earth, he was the future boss of the mafia his father led. At that time, he was the second strongest person on earth, but now he is the most powerful person you could ever imagine.

However, given that I was merely trying to find food and had inadvertently "harmed" this man, anything is possible. That's the only scenario I can envision, as it's unlikely that anyone else could have fallen into the same grave as my mother. It's difficult to pinpoint exactly what he felt, but there must have been a sudden surge of emotion. Like he had gotten to taste a drug, which he later would try to find in me still. Otherwise, he would have let me fall to the ground in that second and be removed by anybody afterwards, not stay as a shadow for years while looking for how I grew up and got as a person.

My father would do everything to get back from his business trip as fast as possible. They were kind enough to let him go back to the funeral a week after my birth. You never saw him cry, smile, or be angry at me for what I had done. He was intelligent enough to understand that I wasn't the murderer, and he never made a cross at the woman who gave birth to me. Regardless of her identity, he buried a piece of his heart in her grave. The small rest, which somehow kept him alive, would make me feel like he was home someday.

Already a day later, he was on the same business trip again. Whose did, for instance, not include noble restaurants, suits, and ties, but most often the substance I got familiar with on my first day on earth? Blood. Harm. Loss. Not that he wasn't a person who bore it; he was a killer and had maybe even more on his list than his boss, but he had a heart too. That was the difference. He possessed this item prior to its removal for safety reasons. I could never trust their claims that there was no chance of saving her. He knew that too. They always chose who to let live or die. My mother was not present in that scene. They chose the second.

Because of his abstinence, another person came closer to watch me. Carlo Gagliardi Faraldo, a mafia boss with a strategic mind and exceptional diplomatic skills, leaves a lasting impression on me every time I see him. At the age of one, that might have been a small thing to consider, but it got a larger one faster than anybody could have expected.

My first touch wouldn't leave any permanent marks on his skin, but something had changed inside him, leading him to choose me immediately. The small little kid, who was glad to walk on its own throughout the year, somehow kept his interest and became part of his future planning. My father wouldn't recognise it. Carlo had been so generous as to offer to secure a nanny for me, but he should exercise caution in the fights outside. Most of the time, my father would be on business trips for around a month or even more. Carlo wouldn't visit me more than once throughout the time. With the age of zero or one day one, you are useless to a mafia boss. However, the fact that I encountered him more frequently than any other male individual left a lasting impression on me. His influence would endure indefinitely.

During the period when he was absent and my father was away on a business trip, I had a caretaker who watched me. The identity of the caretaker was not determined by my father. He was glad that he didn't have to worry about me a lot. The death of his beloved wife harmed his heart more than it should have. Being vulnerable to something that no one understands is a painful experience. Some of the men on the scene have killed their own wives after betraying them. What they got was more acceptance than punishment. My first lesson was to be cold-hearted and unyielding. The phrase "Don't let anybody touch you unless you want them to" implies that you should either fight back if someone touches you or express your desire for them to do so. Especially women, they had been saying to me, would never learn to read me or understand what I was about to say if the words didn't leave my mouth.

Still, I would not get any kind of special treatment from Carlo. At least there was nothing I was unaware of at the time. As soon as he was around, I kept my eyes and ears open. Nobody wants to disappoint a man as he is. Though he never talked much, the few words that left his mouth always had a lot of meaning and were powerful and controlled, as they said. It was sufficient to etch in my memory every single word he spoke.

You will never grow close to a man like him. Anyone who approaches him will be quickly discarded. Information can either be a source of benefit or a source of destruction. One of the most significant differences between Carlo and Sandey, my father, arises here: Carlo consistently emphasizes the importance of keeping an open mind and absorbing as much information as possible, whereas Sandey believes that I should refrain from speaking or acting in a certain way. Sandey was trying to convince me not to listen or ask questions. His motto, "Loyalty is silence, strength is shadows," left me wondering for a long time what he meant by it. It wasn't until I reached a certain age that I understood his purposes.

At first, it was about our family. Secrets and knowledge bind us together, requiring us to remain silent and never explain anything, even in the most challenging situations. We all have to be devoted to our families to survive. If we are not, we face two significant risks of being killed: either by our community, who will perceive our weakness, or by the others, who will torture us until they have all the information they need to kill us. Once you entered such a room, there was no way out. Every promise is a lie.

From all that I have been writing down right now, I have mainly heard about it and been told stories from those around me. As I write this book, I am seventeen, three weeks before my next birthday. I had a strong desire to document everything prior to the ceremony and the final meeting with my parents and the don. In the book, I wanted to repeat my story and get a clearer idea of what to do later in my life. Already, I know that my father has very different ideas of what I could possibly do instead of becoming the next don. I have all of Carlo's support; he has been teaching me well, but in what way will you learn throughout the book? Each chapter represents a single year in my life. Here are the first twelve months, with small pieces of the background story to sum up and understand me. I know it will be hard. I know you can do it. I know that you will do it.

The only video from my birth year is from one of the ceremonies when I was half a year old. It provides a clearer understanding of what I've been told, yet it still leaves me feeling shocked. I have never felt so close or convinced by someone my age before. In the video, the pain of my father is evident in his eyes and facial expressions. The way he holds me makes it seem as though I'm the most important thing he has left. It gave me a new perspective on his world and direction.

"Ladies and gentlemen, esteemed members of our family," the former consignee began his speech. "It is with great honour and pride that I welcome you to this special occasion. Tonight, we gather not for a matter of business or strategy but for something far more precious—the introduction of a new life into our cherished family.

We are here to celebrate the arrival of a young soul, a symbol of our enduring legacy and the bright future that lies ahead. This evening, we welcome Silas Ambrose Farell Farris, *the beloved child of* Sandey Farell Farris *and* Ava Farell Farris.

As we stand together in this sacred hall, let us remember the values that bind us: honour, loyalty, and respect. These are the pillars upon which our family is built, and it is our duty to pass on these principles to the next generation.

Our family is not just a network of individuals but a united force, a fortress of strength and unity. In this spirit, we come together to bless and welcome Silas Ambrose Farell Farris, ensuring that they are surrounded by love, guidance, and the unwavering support of all who stand here today.

Now, I invite Sandey Farell Farris to present the child to our esteemed Don so that we may commence this beautiful ceremony. Let us all gather close and witness the blessing of a new life, the continuation of our proud lineage, and the promise of our shared future. Thank you." Afterwards, he went step by step with me in his arms to Carlo, who looked the same as he does now. They nodded towards each other; my father's eyes red from the hard times after her death. The don stepped closer to us, leaving the rest of the room as silent as a flock of birds following a death. As he held a small gold medallion bearing the family crest and gently placed it on my forehead, he also began to speak. Never have I heard that many words leave his mouth at once. As soon as I heard this for the first time, I immediately wondered if it was something he had done in the past, or if I had already been special to him in some way.

"Today, we gather as one family, bound by blood, honour, and an unbreakable bond. We welcome you, Silas Ambrose Farell Farris, to our world, our hearts, and our legacy.

May you grow strong and wise, with the courage to face all the challenges that life may present. May you carry our name with pride, embodying the values of loyalty, respect, and honour that define us.

This medallion, marked with our family crest, symbolizes our family's strength and unity. As it touches your brow, it is a reminder that you are never alone; you are always protected by those who came before you and those who stand with you now."
While he speaks with a calm voice, he places the medallion on my brow, and in that moment, his face softens for a while. Even if there had been no tension before, he would have a noticeable reaction in that moment.
"May your journey be blessed with prosperity, and may you always find the guidance and support you need within this family. We, the members of this family, pledge to guide, protect, and nurture you with the wisdom of our traditions and the warmth of our love.

Welcome, little one, to the Faraldo family. You are our future, our hope, and our pride. As we gather here today, know that you are cherished beyond measure. May your life be long, your path straight, and your heart loyal to us."

Father nodded to him with a hint of a thankful smile before he raised his glass and looked towards the camera gain. "Salute to Silas Ambrose Farell Farris!" Everybody stood up and applauded me.

The news sent a chill down my spine. Many of them had already died or were "released" from the family. The father had undergone significant changes and had aged considerably. At that time, he was in his mid-twenties, already scarred by the difficult experiences he had faced, yet he was still young.

In the remainder of the video, you will witness all the guests either sitting down or coming to my father to offer their condolences and small gifts. There was everything, from baby clothing to quality food and weapons. He would always remain polite, smile, and give a simple nod. The event itself looked more like one from a large family than a mafia meeting. Whose is different? After I had been a part of the ceremony, I had the right to be at every other feast too. Even if I hadn't caused any harm previously, was this ritual still necessary? They did it as fast as possible in my case, so that my father could bring me to them too, even if he didn't like it at all. There was no other choice for him. He was, after all, merely a close henchman to the don, heavily reliant on his understanding of him and his assistance. All of us strive to return home safely. With the protection of just our family name, it gets easier to do that with just our family name protection. For some, joining the family was a lifelong dream, regardless of their circumstances. Many had grown dependent on serving them in the best way possible. Also, my father.

The first meeting is maybe the earliest experience I remember in my life. Later, it turned into a regular routine, occurring once a month at the same location and time. However, it was particularly special and intense because I had been away from it for only half a year. It was the only time I had been there without being able to leave. The second was that my father had a conflict with the don because he wanted to protect me from the event. Throughout those months, I had learned to walk—not perfectly, but good enough to be able to reject any kind of event more precisely.

The first time, I sat three seats away from the Don, but on the opposite side of my father. He was tense the entire time, watching me as if they could kill me at any moment. They could, but why should they? The place was significantly safer than where he had been sitting with the other "workers." All the men there are brutal, but that is still the norm in the upper class; otherwise, they are the ones who kill and torture daily, often more than one person.

The first memory I have is of Don smiling. He smiled because I started to laugh as one of the men was thrown out of the family for betrayal. I saw nothing but blood, fear, and respect. Everyone stared at me in shock, fearing the consequences of their actions. He approached me and forced me to sit up, giving me a clearer view of the situation. My father's face tensed even more as I realized what I had begged for. Once someone is named, their loyalty and trust to the family diminishes.
They began severing his tongue and inserting it into his mouth, while simultaneously carving the symbol of "trash" into his skull. It had thirteen stripes on each side, making it look like a plaid piece of paper. A bloody piece of paper.

Everyone had been staring at it, and if anyone looked away or felt ashamed, they would likely be the next to do so. It is possible that he would not have taken any action against me if I had not done so; however, I was so captivated that I was unable to look away. The first beat of my heart had been the first beat of a murderer. A cold-hearted, headstrong, but smart killer.

That evening, my father would cry in front of me. I couldn't help but wonder why he did that. Perhaps it was because I didn't resemble him as much as he desired, or perhaps I bore some similarities to his wife. The choices I made aligned with her preferences. One time, counting forever. The way I had come to know Carlo was rational. Others may find it harsh, hard, cruel, or even psycho-like. The way I grew up was something nobody knew. You'll learn about that. Before my life changes completely, you will understand me. Still, I wonder if I should look forward with angriness or pleasure, or as I do now with acceptance.

Chapter 1

"Wake up, boss," my father said to me, and I slowly opened my eyes as he greeted me with a huge smile. So, did I. I almost jumped up to give him a hug. He laughed, but I took him off as fast as possible. Therefore, my earlier smile faded, leading me to believe that I had done something wrong.

"Come, let's eat breakfast together. Afterwards, I had to go to work, which meant that I would be alone again for several weeks or months. Use your time, a voice in my mind said, and so I did. We went downstairs and ate, but we didn't say a word to each other. He was uncomfortable. Since her death, happiness has been an unknown sensation.

"See what I got for you?" He reached me in a play car, and you could see my impressive smile and hear the laughter. Something like a "thank you" left my mouth, but my talking hadn't been that

good for the age of one. I didn't hear many people talking, aside from the professional conversations at the monthly meetings. That was my life. I listened intently and remained silent, attempting to comprehend their words. For a moment, my father continued to smile, but then he glanced at his watch and grabbed the camera, stating that he had to leave.

What transpired after these two video clips is a marvel that I can still vividly recall. Perhaps it didn't have as much of an impact on me in my later life. However, after my father's departure, I would finish breakfast with my caretaker, with the intention of using the rest of the day to try out a new play. I accepted that he was away again, for how long I didn't know.

It surprised me as the door opened again. I thought that my father had forgotten anything and ran immediately to the door. As I saw who it was, I stood still at once, looking at him in wonder, with small hints of fear but also delight.

"My don," I uttered, my gaze fixed on the ground, as he stepped closer to me. All I could see were his feet. My heartbeat was so fast that it almost ached. I had seen what he had done before, and it had both shocked and fascinated me. Particularly, I was fascinated by the reaction of the person who received punishment, while the other person was at a loss for words. Today, I understand that their pain stems from witnessing one person's death, and they harbour a deep-seated hatred towards him for his betrayal. It's been a long time since I witnessed that last half-year, but such images never truly fade from memory. At least it's not mine. I am not a person who forgets. As a result, I have not been trained. Contrary to that time, I wouldn't get rest now. It's not because you're traumatised, but rather because you're unaware of what's going on around you in this state of powerlessness.

"Sit," he said, and I went to my chair, sitting down carefully. I had never looked him directly in the eyes before. I never looked at his face at all, since I knew that his eyes were on me. I scanned everything I did. Each inhalation, stride, heartbeat, feeling, and response was scrutinized.

He sat down in front of me while I looked at his hands. He was holding a small box in his hand. The cold, hard plastic shell was black with waves. At once, I became more interested in it, my eyes widening in wonder at what it was.

"Open," he slid it slowly towards me, but at once it came closer, and my eyes widened in happiness. At that time, I knew him well enough from the few meetings to be sure that he wouldn't give me any bullshit. He wasn't a man who wasted his time, nor was he one who wasted his money. He was not your typical mafia boss, but rather the greatest he had known for centuries.

Slowly, I opened each side lock and looked at the item inside. Without saying anything, I took it out of my hands, which were large enough to surround the cold grip.

"It's a replica of the Kongsberg Colt M 1914," he said, causing my smile to widen. Despite not pressing the shooting button, I tried to act like I could shoot with it, just as I had seen them do in the past. He nodded and took it out of my hands.

"Don't approach it as if it's a delicate matter. It's hot, but you have to play with it, not against it". Perhaps there was a hint of fear brewing within me. Even though I hadn't seen such items in use before that day, they already had a powerful aura. You don't need to witness someone's death to understand its potency. The idea that, if I were to steer it, it wouldn't be the items, but rather my kill.

He would reach for the item again, smiling with amusement as I held it correctly the next time I tried it. What had seemed hard was now easy. I could do it. That was what I would be trained for. That was the purpose of my life.

Otherwise, then my father I wouldn't waste a single tear to be closer to the family. I wanted it. Even had already illuminated me at such a young age, even if I had no idea what I would get myself into.

"It's not loaded, nor is it a real weapon. This is the ammunition. He placed it on the table, and I immediately set down the pistol, eager to insert some of the small plastic balls into it. He observed my actions without uttering a word but corrected me when I mistakenly placed it in the incorrect location.

My first shot was taken against the floor, just inches away from my own feet. He immediately reacted, removing the object from my hands and instructing me on how to direct my shot. That was how the remainder of my first birthday evening unfolded. I thoroughly enjoyed the experience, even though he had to caution me towards the end.

"As long as your father is away, you can do whatever you want while not shooting at yourself. As soon as he returns, hide it. Alright, I nodded enthusiastically, relishing the prospect of a new task that might be the first I truly enjoyed and found meaningful.

One and a half months later, my father was back from work. As I watched him approach, his hands were still drenched in blood. Even though he attempted to conceal it, the moment he caught sight of me, my awareness sharpened. I did realise everything at once. However, I would still retreat as soon as he entered the bathroom, allowing me to conceal my new weapon in my own room. At this age, I already had this ability, as my father couldn't tolerate seeing me for more than a few hours a day and needed the night to rest. Otherwise, working outside would be too dangerous for him. However, there was always a sense of missing something.

"Have you eaten?" he asked as he came out, and I exited my room slowly.

"Yes, there is still something in the kitchen." He nodded but failed to understand that I wanted to spend time with him, regardless of what he would do while we were together. For me, he wasn't a fascinating man. He was a weak man, unwilling to look at his own son or fight like others would. Following the death of his wife, he continued to work diligently, even when I was still living at home. It wasn't my fault, he said, but still, I felt like the last beat of her heart switched to being the first of mine. All of her strength and power seemed to overwhelm my small frame. Regrettably, I didn't acquire the knowledge on my own.

He got me into bed just five minutes after he entered the door. I lay there, longing for him to leave me once more.

"Father," I said, and a visible shadow ran through his spine as he turned around to face me again. His heart was beating faster than mine in that moment.

"Could you read or tell me a goodnight story?" He frowned while opening his mouth to argue.

"I am not a good storyteller," he explained as I smiled and gently tapped the mattress next to me, symbolizing his approach and beginning.

After pondering for some time, he slowly approached me, maintaining the same smile. He sat down beside me, his head in his hands, desperately trying to come up with something to say.

"I can tell you a personal story." I nodded, prepared to listen. He shrugged, as if he were giving up the struggle to never do that and started speaking. His voice, despite "not being a good storyteller," immediately calmed me as he spoke about his unfortunate past. Throughout the rest of the year, I heard the entire story.

"My childhood is the most beautiful memory I have. My parents were caring and protective, didn't support anything illegal, and went to church with me at least once a week or more. I would learn to appreciate it, even if I never believed in anything that I hadn't seen. However, as I grew closer to their community and began to visit their cloisters, I discovered something that immediately ignited my passion—a story I will share with you later." Later, I would lie down and reflect on his words. It made me wonder how life in the other world was, even if I liked my life the way it was there too.

His story continued for many evenings, covering everything from small details from strangers I would never get to know to huge events I would never get to be part of. Twisted feelings lingered inside me; the other world seemed suddenly more interesting, but never enough to make me say it aloud. I only listened, as always.

"My family lived a vegetarian lifestyle for many years as I worked at the monastery. The fact that they used to grow many different herbs, fruits, and berries wasn't unusual for me. However, one particular person captured my attention. Although she was undoubtedly in her eighties at the time, her support for her own thoughts and opinions was evident. I was just a little boy back then, maybe not even a teenager. However, I had already decided to take action, fulfilling a promise I had made to her on the day of her death. Perhaps that was the last thing she heard before she took her final breath. Years later, I would become a journalist. There are top-notch degrees available everywhere, and I receive recommendations for the top universities both domestically and globally. Ultimately, I began my studies near my hometown, conducting research and writing articles on the theme that inspired me. The pharmaceutical industry is against natural healing. The pharmaceutical industry produces medications that are ineffective and originate from the most unfavourable places. Their expertise lies solely in marketing. One day, he would say, "That was what got me into the harshest problems you can imagine," sparking my interest. I had never heard about anything like that. I understood, but after my few months on earth, I never considered it of any further importance for my later life. Nevertheless, it deeply resonated with me and shaped my personal path.

"Carlo, who saved me after they kidnapped and tortured me for several months, is the reason I'm here. He promised to make it appear as though I had an accident, but for some reason, he brought me here and retrained me. Regrettably, he failed to factor in your mother's influence". My father laughed while tears left his eyes. "A wonderful, smart, and stubborn woman," he said, shaking his head with a smile. "She found me somehow, while she always knew that I was alive. Her abilities are special. Everything she felt was more intense, sometimes to the point where I worried about her, and other times it would save us from a forever-lasting separation." His eyes were honest and softened while he thought about her. The sensation that I was her now resides deep within me. That was what I had been thinking about for years before learning about genetics.

"She became pregnant with you half a year after we moved in together alone." Perhaps it stemmed from the intense meetings we had, followed by my return from work. He laughed, leaving me to ponder why we would never celebrate his arrival.

You may be familiar with the rest of the story. She was pregnant with you, and while I tried to be home as often as possible, she was mostly alone and didn't have it easy. "No woman in our world has it easy, Jake," he said, using my grandfather's name. He used to refer to me by this name because my mother had chosen my real name, which he found uncomfortable to say out loud.

"Please don't ever become like them. Try to stay away as long as possible, even if I can't always be here. It would be ideal for you to have a happy childhood, free from their manipulation and traditions. You can be sure that if I had a choice, I would never have come here. "I may be a journalist and volunteer in the cloister while still being a happy family man," he said, swallowing deeply at the last word. Children may not express themselves often and may appear to receive little, but they do receive much. I did. Immediately, I realized that while I might be his son and part of his family, I was never enough for him. His heart had suffered too much to accept a single person as plaster.

The good-night stories would most often end in tears. Not me, but him. Over the course of this year, I was absent from every single family gathering. I enjoyed it, as I have a strong affinity for people. I hated being alone, and that one time in a month made me look forward to something again.
Additionally, I would get visits from Carlo once a week when my father wasn't home. He taught me how to shoot and took the time to explain the setup of everything, how you clean it, and what you shouldn't do with a gun. Years later, as my father was on a work-trip again, he would even give me his own gun to practice my first real shot, a gesture of appreciation for my quick learning. After I pressed it, the power was so intense that I fell back. Still, he was proud of me. Then what I had shouted was nothing else, and I should shoot into the middle of the huge round target. My eyes were there, shining, and I had no idea how much this ability would make me suffer and save my life in the future.

Chapter 2

My father had been at work for almost two months. Today was my birthday. I was alone.

I recall hoping that Carlo would at least come once to do something with me. Just anything. In the end, it was nothing. What does a child do when they are alone for such a long period of time? It gets creative. Of course, the babysitter would give me some food twice a day, but otherwise they would mainly just "be there," but never for me.

I took what I found—a rope. Using this, I tried to create beautiful knots. The first was simple and boring, but as the hours passed, I got satisfied with my work. It really did not look like the work of a two-year-old child, but when did I ever get the time to be that anyway?

It wasn't until a week later that Carlo would come to me. When I saw him, I had to stop myself from hugging him in joy. He didn't say anything to me about what was happening, but I was so happy to ask anyway.

"You are able to go, walk, run, stand still, and move with the rest of your body, as I see. At your age, I began with more challenging tasks, but we can now start with anything." I nodded, not eagerly because I knew he wouldn't like it, but because I controlled my emotions to show my gladness without being overly happy.

"We start with Tai Chi," he said. Without that, I knew what Tai Chi was, but I would learn more. I remember my first lesson very well. The instructor was an older man. We would start with a greeting and a brief explanation, and he assured me several times that we would do some fun, gentle movements together to feel like a calm and strong tree. It may have been the first time anyone treated me more like a child.

The warm-up lasted about five minutes, which was about as long as the greeting. We'd do breathing exercises there. I had to stand with my feet shoulder-width apart, place my hands on my tummy, and take deep breaths in and out. We'd also do some gentle stretching, such as reaching up to the sky (stretching arms upward) and touching toes (bending forward).

Afterwards, we would start with the basic movements. It really was fun, even if it may sound boring. For me, just the attention was illuminating.

The tai chi walk demonstrated slow, exaggerated steps, placing one foot carefully in front of the other. Encourage me to walk like a slow, quiet tiger. By practicing, I would learn more about how to move my arms in slow, flowing motions, akin to "painting a rainbow" in the air. Most fun are the animal movements. That could mean anything from standing on one leg and gently flapping arms like a crane to making slow, heavy steps while swaying side to side like a bear.

Ultimately, the teacher believed that cooling down in any manner was crucial. For example, I was standing with feet wide apart, and arms rounded in front, as if encircling a tree trunk. This helped me with grounding and balance. After such a session, it was also important to return to the simple breathing exercise from the warm-up, promoting calmness and relaxation.

Throughout the entire process, but especially towards the end, he would lavish me with praise, far more than I was accustomed to. It may have been hard since I wasn't used to any praise at all, but it was still supportive of my motivation. In the end, we made the closing ritual, which was a slight bow to show respect while we thanked each other for the time. I would have it almost every day, as long as my father was away. I loved it. Finally, I didn't have to come upon anything myself.

Carlo would visit me twice a month, while my father came another month later but wouldn't stay longer than two weeks. I didn't feel sad about that. I loved my sports, but I could only do the "fun stuff," then he was away anyway. Twice a month, shooting with Carlo; otherwise, training every single day. It may seem like a lot, but I learned fast, and progress is motivating. This is particularly true when you have no other tasks to complete.

After three months, Carlo would tell me that staying at one thing for such a long time wasn't beneficial and encourage me to move forward. I continued to take lessons with the same teacher, but in a different manner. It was called "Qi Gong.".

As always, we began with our usual greetings, and he explained to me for the first time what this would do to me.

"It will make you feel both calm and strong, like a wise turtle." I would laugh at his explanations as we restarted the warm-up, which was very similar to the previous one with breathing and stretching techniques.

Afterwards, I gained an understanding of the differences. At the start, it was more about breathing; Jarle, my teacher, would hold an imaginary balloon in front of my mouth. Encourage me to take a deep breath in to fill the balloon, and then gently blow the air out to deflate it. He showed me other ways to move my arms in a slow, flowing motion, like gently waving clouds in the sky or swimming like a "dragon" through the air, using slow and deliberate arm movements. I loved his descriptions of the smallest events, even though I may have felt like a child. At the end of our sessions, we would again praise ourselves and do the same goodbye routine that we had encouraged.

Luckily, my father would again be far away. I would get a lot of time to practice and train, and somehow, I felt that Carlo was proud of me. The way he nodded towards me, as if I had done something right, made me feel that I had done it very well, even though he never said so.

This time, not more than one or one and a half months had passed before we started with the next exercise, karate.

Now, I would begin with something that eventually became a larger part of me, providing me with a sense of freedom and wellbeing. Running. At that time, it was only seen as a warm-up, but it later became much more to me.

Afterwards, I had to stand on one leg and switch to the other one, like a tree swaying in the wind. He would also show me how to gently roll on the mat from my back to my belly and back again. As a two and a half-year-old child, I found it effortless, and his lack of flexibility at that age inspired me. Spoiler: Even if I trained as much as possible, I wouldn't remain that way either.

He held my hands and gently guided me through basic movements, such as stepping to the side, turning, or performing arm movements like a waterfall. He would once again persuade me through all the simulations, just as he had done with Tai Chi and Qi Gong.

Otherwise, we would sit down and practice quiet time, while I had to close my eyes and take deep breaths. In the end, we would also stretch out and establish a routine for saying goodbye.

I wouldn't recommend sticking with this for more than a month before transitioning to Aikido. It was similar in structure but not fully aligned with the other lessons. Again, I would start by running, but later practice my balance more. This could involve standing on one leg and then switching to the other, akin to a flamingo stance. We also practiced the same rolling techniques, albeit in different ways and on different sides. Jarle would also hold my hands and gently guide me through my turning movements. Initially, I found it difficult to encourage others to exercise, but as I continued to practice, I understood its significance.

Additionally, we would do step-and-move exercises with my favourite imaginaries. There were animal movements there, and I had to pretend to be anything he pointed out and move around the room, simulating it. The session ended with quiet time, stretching, and our usual goodbyes.

The primary reason I am skimming through it so quickly right now is because we didn't engage in this activity for a few months. My father would come back once and stay for an entire month at home before he went to work again. I almost begged him to go earlier, and I missed everything a lot, but he never knew about it anyway. It was just something between Carlo, Jarle, and me. I had to remain vigilant once he arrived, but I also understood that it was a test to see if I could trust him sufficiently.

The last activity we started two months before my next birthday was called "dim mak," which involves precise knowledge of vital points and is not suitable for toddlers due to safety concerns. Therefore, we would initially focus on activities that promote safety, fun, and basic martial arts principles appropriate for toddlers before moving on to more harmful vital points and movements.

The warm-up was based on my animal movements, but that was one of the only things that remained similar to the other types of lessons.

At the first training, we would start with gentle kicking and punching motions, making sure to emphasise control and safety. Over time, this would become increasingly challenging, sometimes pushing me to my limits.

We would also start by pretending to be a ninja, which included both sneaking and hiding. That was a lesson I loved and grew much better at. It didn't take many lessons before I could walk without making any sound or, in the end, even run without doing so. As a result, Jarle gave me his nickname: Sneaking Pantheon.

Finally, we would conclude with some breathing exercises and our customary farewells. We would do a mixture of every time we met after a month of training. It was challenging and frustrating not to share my success with my father. He would inquire about my activities, to which I would respond with drawings I had hastily completed before his arrival or mention that I had played with the car he had given me for my birthday. Fortunately, he was disinterested enough not to dwell on it.

The meetings with Carlo are still the high point of my month. It wasn't necessarily about the shooting; rather, it was about learning from him. He taught me not just the art of handling a gun but also the importance of his presence. At that time, he was clearly my idol, even if I never tried to please him. Something inside me always told me that doing so would be wrong. I had witnessed numerous instances where individuals attempted to do so, failed, and were immediately dismissed as soon as someone noticed their attempt. The difference lies in the fact that my attention span is not compromised. I simply aspired to emulate him, but at that time, I didn't comprehend the actions of others or what it meant to "be like him."

"We have to finish earlier today; your father will be back this afternoon," Carlo mentioned, and my face fell. It might have looked alike. Although I didn't harbour hatred for my father, he remained silent about it. He would simply glance around to ensure we didn't cause any harm. Everything was fine. I had become a good shooter. Even when we practiced indoors, the rain was a hindrance. Over the past few weeks, I have almost never been able to practice outside, despite the fact that it would have been even more beneficial to have more distance to challenge myself.

Following his instructions, I sat silently and began cleaning the weapon. Regardless of the fact that it was merely a toy pistol, I consistently cleaned it. My mood wasn't the best in that moment; I was sad because my training hadn't lasted as long as I wished, and I wasn't sure when I would have it again since I never knew how long dad would stay.

"Your birthday is in a few weeks." I looked up, not meeting his eyes but just showing a reaction so that it wouldn't look like I ignored him.

"It is nothing special," I said, almost in a self-petite manner, as I could still feel their gaze on me.

"Ageing is only something bad for people my age." His final words before he left me alone again were, "I become weaker; you get stronger day by day; think about that." I wonder if I have been thinking about them for days, weeks, months, or even years. Still, I never got to a conclusion about what it would mean for me.

On one side, he would acknowledge that while he was getting older and possibly weaker, I was growing and becoming stronger each day. This would positively contribute to my growth and inspire me to value my own progress and power even more.

It offers a perspective on ageing; it made me understand that getting older can come with challenges, but it also signifies the wisdom and experience that the older person has. It may encourage me to value and respect the aging process and the knowledge that comes with it, while also making me understand the natural cycle of life, where the younger generation grows stronger and takes on new roles as the older generation gradually steps back. It is a gentle way to introduce the concept of aging and responsibilities shifting over time.

However, it never escaped my mind that Carlo might have been attempting to establish an emotional bond, implying that despite his physical decline, he derives joy and pride from witnessing my growth and strength. It suggests a passing of the torch, where the elder finds fulfilment in the younger generation's progress.

Overall, the statement was empowering for me. It acknowledges the inevitable changes that come with aging, while I started focusing on the child's positive growth and strength. It encourages me to think about their own development and the potential they have to grow stronger and more capable each day.

At least that was my conclusion over the years. I continue to focus on the idea that there is no inherent right or wrong in this statement. Yet I felt it. This was particularly evident during my days of solitude. Step by step, I grew stronger, more powerful, and smarter. I felt like running, but there was an obstacle in front of me. I may not have noticed it until the door opened and I had to jump up, the weapon still in my hand.

Chapter 3

I never jumped up faster. Never had I run away faster, nor had I ever hidden the weapon faster than in that moment, when my father entered the house all of a sudden.

Afterwards, I would run back to him, but stop right in front so that he would not notice the unusual behaviour. After three months of abstinence, who would have thought it was normal for us to give him a hug? I would greet him with a firm "hello" and give him a brief moment of focus, after which he would need to take a break from me. I was never a complicated child; it was always more about remembering his wife when he saw me.

"What did you do the past few months?" he asked, and I looked around the house while searching for anything I would have done without my lessons. He wouldn't be pleased if I said that Carlo had visited me, even if I held my tongue about why he would do it and what we did while he was here. Neither would he jump up in delight if I told him about my courses or how much progress I had made in such a short amount of time.

"I played with the car you gave me, looked through some of the books, and drew a little more," I said. He nodded, and with that, the most complicated question was finished. I wondered if he really believed in it, or if it was just enough to calm himself from whatever else I could have done. Partly, I was not lying. I had been examining some of the books; their themes were a mystery to him. On the other side, what did he expect? The mixture of an intellectual critic and a stubborn, headstrong woman makes a weak child who enjoys playing with a single car for three months.

The following day, we would go to the next family meeting together. I struggled to keep my eyes off Carlo as I sat in the middle of the room, as far away from my father as possible. Beside me were the other youngest members. Both of them were not at all interested in me until now, but a little spoiler: that would change. Everything would change.

"Buonasera, amici. Tonight, we come together not only as a family but also as the leaders of an empire. Our influence stretches far and wide, and our actions echo through every corner of the world. It's our responsibility to ensure that our power remains unchallenged and our legacy endures." Carlo began by looking at each member; only a few would dare look anywhere else than on the table in front of them, while everybody listened closely to the words that left his mouth.

The consigliere nodded in agreement, stepping forward before he started to talk too.

"We have several important matters to discuss. First, our expansion into new territories. The operations in Europe are progressing smoothly, but there are some concerns about resistance from local factions. We must strengthen our alliances and maintain our unwavering presence.

Our men in Paris have reported increased police activity. It seems the authorities are tightening their grip. We need to consider whether to lay low for a while or to assert our dominance more forcefully. I suggest demonstrating our strength to remind them who is in charge of the streets.

Yes, strength, but with precision. We cannot afford unnecessary attention. Increase our security and ensure our operations are clean. Let them see our power through actions, not just our presence. Move the vulnerable assets to safer locations and reinforce our loyal partners." The other person nodded while I looked for a short second in the other direction. My father sat there, tense, not looking at me or anyone else. He stared at the table, seemingly calculating for himself the implications of the upcoming conversation. As I turned around again, another man started to calmly explain his point of view.

"The situation in South America is also evolving. The new political climate could either be an opportunity or a threat. We need to decide how to position ourselves to take advantage of any shifts in power. Our contacts there are ready to act on our command." I was watching Carlo, trying to gauge his reaction, when he suddenly turned to face me. As our eyes met for the first time ever, my first intension was to look away, but on the other side, it would appear that I had done anything illegal. Therefore, I held eye contact for a few seconds, which made my heart beat faster than the sound of a herd of running horses.

The man nodded thoughtfully, glancing back at the other person before he began to speak.

"Politics is a game we know well. Use our influence to support candidates who align with our interests. And if they win, ensure they remember who helped them rise to power. Keep our operations adaptable; we need to be ready to pivot as the situation demands." While he was saying that, I stopped staring at him, almost afraid to meet his eyes again. They were there, as ominous as the night and as perilous as stepping into a fire. Just by glancing at them, I understood the respect everyone would have for him, even if they had killed so many people before. Even the strongest man I have ever seen in the Mafia family would kneel down to kiss his feet instead of harming him in any way.

The consignee cleared his throat once more, glanced at the don, and then addressed the entire room. "Lastly, there's the matter of internal affairs. Trust and loyalty within our ranks are paramount. There have been whispers of dissent, minor as they may be. We need to address this before it grows. Loyalty is rewarded, but betrayal will not be tolerated." As images of blood, fear, and hopelessness ran through my mind, a shiver ran through my spine. It wasn't just me; in that moment, everyone would glance at the table, hoping that no one close to them or even their family was present. If the last one was the case, the don would check it out too. It was more common for a large group, usually their family, to strive for power rather than just one individual.

Carlo stood up, exuding authority and finality, while no one breathed, fearing that he might look upon them and consider their betrayal. It was an honour for everyone to have protection and be part of this family, but it also meant the fear of being judged.

"Let it be known: our family thrives on loyalty, honour, and respect. We are stronger together than apart. Anyone who questions their place in this family must remember the price of disloyalty. But for those who remain true, our support is unwavering, our bond unbreakable." A brief sigh escaped their lips as they realised that no one would perish today. It was a warning, not the start of a bloody evening. Afterwards, everybody looked up again. While he paused and gazed into each member's eyes, he also searched for those who wouldn't tolerate it, often identifying them as liars. Yes, it was intimidating, but on the other hand, no one would leave the family until they witnessed a betrayal.

"We have weathered many storms, and we will continue to rise above any challenge. Our family is our strength. Let us proceed with clarity, determination, and unity. To our continued success. Salute!" He said it louder, and everybody raised their glasses as a single word from them made the entire room vibrate and echo.

"Salute!" they all exclaimed, and Carlo's unreadable smile made me shiver once more. Afterwards, he would sit down again, signalling the end of the formal dress code. "Now, let us get to work". He concluded, "We have an empire to run," before everyone stood up and left the room one by one. As I attempted to pass him, he extended his hand to block my path.

"Remember, your character's strength shines through your eyes. When you meet someone's eyes with confidence, you share a silent message of self-assurance and mutual respect. It's in these unspoken moments that true understanding and connection are born. Let your eyes reflect your inner courage and integrity." Before I could answer, my father stood by my side. Their eyes would meet; may my father, as strong as his heart was after his wife's death, be the only person who was strong enough to look Carlo in the eyes for hours without being traumatised to death afterwards.

"Is there anything important, my don?" he inquired, wrapping a supportive arm around my shoulders. I gazed down at the ground, detesting their confrontation. Both sides showed me another kind of life from which I could choose, but until now, I had no idea what it would mean for me in the end.

"Too much, Sandey," was what Carlo said while I stiffened in fear of running away. Something was lingering in the air; I knew it, and it made me feel like something new should come soon. I wondered if I had to fear it or look forward to finding out whatever it might be.

"Jake, please go home; I have to talk with him for a few minutes alone. I will be back home this evening," my father said, and I looked into Carlo's eyes once more, wondering if he would support what we had done or leave it like it was and give up. His assuring nod made me know that he would fight, but my father's hardening hand also let me know that he would not give up.

I stood there, between the most influential people in my life, and I had to let them be alone without me. Whatever they would say in the near future would shape a new path for my life, which I would have to follow. In the end, I was only three years old, since today was the day of my birth. That was why they would have this conversation—not to celebrate but to plan how the next year would look. Before we went away from home this morning, I noticed at least one thing: the gun had been touched since I polished it. My father had been in my room while I was asleep.

Half a year later, I woke up as another person. Each step I had to take was planned; at least it felt alike. Carlo had persuaded my father to accept or at least engage in a negotiation, despite my father's reluctance to let his influence affect me. On the other hand, he was not stupid and understood my support for his idea of breaking our contact, as well as the fact that, realistically, it was not possible if he didn't want to.

My father had insisted that I undergo training in all five sports, in addition to learning reading, writing, language, and math. A typical day in my life now consisted of physical training with Jarle, receiving private education from Steve, and concluding with another training session, which occasionally included shooting practice. I would leave the house at exactly six a.m. each day and be back at eight p.m. to eat and get some rest before the days would continue like that again. That helped everyone; my father didn't have to see me more than he wanted, and I could train as hard as I could to fulfill the enormous potential inside me. Meanwhile, Carlo continued to watch me closely and pay for everything, with the intention of extracting something from me every day. I couldn't imagine what exactly he wanted these days, but my father was well aware of it, which may have been the only reason he didn't like the whole setup.

My own problem, or benefit, was that I liked everything in which I participated each day. My father's genetics may have contributed to my desire to learn as much as possible. In the course of a few months, I had learned to read and partly to write, and I had to practice a lot on the look of my handwriting. Additionally, we started with three languages at once. I practice English as my mother tongue more since it is a global language that might later help me with international business, finances, and trading. Additionally, a significant portion of scientific research, technological innovation, and academic literature is published in English. This underscored the significance of improving my grammar and speaking fluency. As I previously mentioned, I wasn't accustomed to conversing frequently. Even though I had some of the longest conversations with Jarle, it didn't make me a better speaker.

Additionally, I learned Mandarin Chinese, since China has the second-largest economy in the world and is a major player in global trade and business. It is also the most spoken language in the world by native speakers, which would provide me with the possibility to talk to over a billion people, enhancing personal and professional connections. The rich history and cultural heritage, heavily influenced by the mafia, piqued my interest. Perhaps this is why

Carlo encouraged me to learn Mandarin, deepening my understanding and appreciation of Chinese culture, philosophy, literature, and traditions.

Additionally, Spanish is widely spoken in many regions where the Mafia has interests, including parts of the United States, Latin America, and Spain. Many drug trafficking routes and organised crime networks operate in Spanish-speaking countries. Knowing Spanish makes it easier to communicate with partners in the drug trade and other illicit activities in these regions. My father appreciated the advantages of knowing Spanish for business and trade in these regions, as well as in the United States, where Spanish is the second most spoken language.

The final subject was something my father strongly discouraged me from learning, but Carlo discreetly removed it from my list as well. Italian. The Mafia has its roots there, particularly in Sicily, Calabria, and Campania. Many traditional Mafia families and operations are Italian or have Italian roots, which we have to cooperate with or fight against. Knowing Italian allows for direct communication with key figures, understanding cultural nuances, and accessing historical and contemporary Mafia literature and codes. However, it also has similarities with Spanish, which wouldn't make the learning all too hard.

Throughout the year, I gained a wealth of knowledge and made both Carlo and my father proud of my progress in math and writing. Since we haven't spoken much, if at all, and my time has been limited, he may not have noticed the progress in my speaking, which has now been greatly influenced by all of the languages I've learned.

Even if Steve had assured me that it would be clearer which language I was talking about as I got more familiar with each, right now my English would be a mixture of the other three languages I learned. Others might find it amusing, but I find it stressful and challenging as I strive for perfection.

There, I didn't face any problems, as all I had to deal with was conflict. Jarle once said to me, "You are a born killer," evoking a range of emotions within me as I grappled with whether I wanted to be the one returning home with blood on my hands. However, our training primarily focused on techniques to protect myself and escape quickly without causing harm.

One day, I had the ability to escape from Jarle; without it, I had to move quickly. He wouldn't catch me as I swung myself under his legs to reach the other side and continue my escape. The action occurred so unexpectedly that it took him a few seconds to comprehend the situation before he could pursue me.

Step by step, I became more dangerous and faster than anyone else, which helped me in many significant ways—I was brainier than most kids my age. Carlo would notice, but he would never rest upon it. Don't let anything remain the way it is just because it is good enough for the moment. My next challenge was already knocking on the door.

Chapter 4

"There's no school for you today. We are taking whose hours for something else," Carlo said at once as he entered my training room, where I had been practicing Dim Mak today. Jarle and I would both look at the watch at the same time, and yes, our early session would have been over in ten minutes.

"Thank you for the lessons today." We both made a bow towards each other while I hurried to change my clothing as fast as possible so that the don wouldn't have to wait for me.

"We are going to our real place for the shooting practices. That will be a benefit, which wouldn't have been possible before your father knew it." I already envisioned myself standing in the midst of the most dangerous men, desperately trying to shoot straight with my play-pistole. I didn't know if I liked the thought. One was a new challenge, and another was a laughing shock.

My worry was unfounded, as I realized that Carlo also didn't want to be seen here with me, especially since the entire building was locked. However, this day will remain in my memory forever.

"I pushed open the heavy glass doors of the shooting hall, my footsteps echoing on the polished marble floor. The lobby was modern and inviting, with sleek lines and a neutral colour palette. It exuded a sense of professionalism and class. Carlo walked beside me, his presence commanding the attention of the staff, who welcomed us with respectful nods.

"Welcome, Mr. Gagliardi. Mr. Farell," the receptionist said, handing us each a key card and a pair of electronic earmuffs. "Your lanes are prepared."

Carlo nodded, a small smile playing on his lips as he gestured for me to follow him. We passed the pro shop, where an array of gleaming firearms and accessories were displayed. Despite the luxury around me, my excitement was tinged with a sense of respect. This was no ordinary shooting range.

As we stepped through the automatic doors into the main hall, I was struck by its sheer size and meticulous design. The hall stretched out before us with a hundred meters of pristine shooting lanes, each separated by ballistic-rated dividers that provided both safety and privacy. The ceilings were at least five meters high, giving the space an airy, open feel. The entire area was illuminated by bright, even lighting, with individual lane lights focusing on the targets. Soft backlighting behind the targets provided perfect visibility.

Carlo led me to lane five, placing his gear on the spotless counter. I followed suit, setting my equipment beside his. Feeling a bit nervous, I pulled out my play-pistol, the one I had practiced with countless times. It felt light and familiar in my hands, a comfort in an unfamiliar environment.

Carlo turned to me, a mix of amusement and seriousness in his eyes. "Silas, put that away," he said, pointing at my toy. "Today, you're going to shoot like a real man." He opened his case and pulled out a sleek, silver handgun. "Here, use mine. This is a Colt 1911. It's reliable and accurate. Perfect for your first time."

I hesitated, but the weight of the real pistol in my hand was reassuring, if not a little intimidating. Carlo stepped closer, his demeanour calm and instructive.

"First, let's talk about your stance," Carlo began, adjusting my posture. "Stand with your feet shoulder-width apart. Keep your knees slightly bent. You want to be stable but flexible."

I followed his instructions, feeling a bit awkward but determined to get it right. Carlo continued, "Now, grip the pistol firmly but not too tight. Your dominant hand should hold the grip, and your other hand should support it. Like this." He demonstrated the proper grip, and I mimicked his movements.

"Good," he said, nodding in approval. "Now, align the sights. The front sight should be centred on the rear sight. Focus on the front sight, not the target. And if you can, keep both eyes open." I took a deep breath, aligning the sights as he had instructed. My heart was

pounding, but I felt a growing sense of confidence with Carlo's guidance.

"Remember to breathe," Carlo advised. "Inhale slowly, then exhale halfway and hold your breath. This will help steady your aim. When you're ready, gently squeeze the trigger. Don't jerk it."

I inhaled, then exhaled halfway, holding my breath. I focused on the front sight and gently squeezed the trigger. The gun fired with a loud bang, and the recoil was surprising but manageable. I hit the target—not dead centre, but close enough.

"Not bad for your first shot," Carlo said, a hint of pride in his voice. "You did well. Now, let's try a few more."

With each shot, Carlo offered more advice. "Adjust your grip slightly... Keep your elbows bent. Breathe, Silas, don't forget to breathe." His instructions were clear and patient, and with each round, I felt more and more confident.

After a few rounds, I paused to inspect my results. The bullet trap at the end of my lane had efficiently captured my shots, and the target system quickly brought the paper back to me. I was pleased with my accuracy at such a long distance, a testament to both my growing skills and Carlo's expert guidance.

As we took a break, Carlo led me to the waiting area, where comfortable seating and refreshments awaited. We sat down, and *he began to talk about the importance of precision and discipline, not just in shooting but in life.*

"You know, Silas," Carlo said, his tone reflective, "this place isn't just about shooting. It's about focus, control, and respect. The way we handle a gun says a lot about how we handle our responsibilities." I nodded, understanding the deeper meaning behind his words. After a brief rest, we returned to the lanes. The advanced facilities, training rooms equipped with AV systems for workshops, and high-tech shooting simulators offered a glimpse into the meticulous attention to detail that characterized everything Carlo did.

Before leaving, Carlo and I shared a moment of quiet reflection. The hall had exceeded all my expectations, providing an unparalleled shooting experience. It wasn't just a place to shoot; it was a sanctuary for those who cherished the art of precision and the thrill of hitting the mark.

As we walked out, I couldn't help but feel a sense of pride and satisfaction. The shooting hall's sheer size and sophistication illuminated not just the targets before us but also the deeper values that Carlo had imparted. The Range of Legends wasn't just about hitting the bullseye; it was about living a life of focus and respect, guided by the principles that made the Gagliardi family the most powerful in the world."

Spoiler alert: it wouldn't be the final shoot, nor would it be the last time we prioritized anything else. We would usually take one of the fighting lessons later. In the end, I got what I looked forward to every week. Yes, you have read right. **Every week,** Carlo would take the time to teach me to shoot like a "real man," which he always pointed out. I quickly forgot about my play-pistole and instead had the opportunity to test a variety of weapons. Carlo allowed me to try everything from the Glock 17, Smith & Wesson M&P Shield, Sig Sauer P226 to Heckler & Koch USP, the Desert Eagle, or a CZ 75 SP-01 Shadow throughout the year. Even if some of them really did not suit my height, even if I was quite tall for my age, he supported me so that it would be possible in the end.

Once a month, we had to skip our meeting for the real family appointment. In addition to the special invitation to one family, we also extended an invitation to another family, recognizing their potential for cooperation. Because of this, only half of our usual count of men was present.

The atmosphere in the dimly lit room was tense, filled with the weight of unspoken tensions and whispered alliances. I stood beside Carlo, observing the meeting between our family and the rival Montini family. It was a delicate dance of power and diplomacy, where words were carefully chosen and gestures held hidden meanings.

But amidst the adults' negotiations, my attention was drawn to a figure seated across the table from me. He was Giovanni Montini, the twelve-year-old son of the Montini family's patriarch. With his sharp eyes and confident demeanour, he exuded an air of authority beyond his years. It was clear that one day he would inherit his family's empire and continue their legacy of power and influence.

As the meeting progressed, Giovanni's gaze lingered on me, his expression unreadable. I felt a surge of unease, a sense that he saw me as more than just a curious bystander. I tried to ignore his scrutiny, focusing instead on Carlo's words and the subtle nuances of the negotiation.

Unexpectedly, Giovanni spoke up. "And who is this?" he asked, his tone tinged with curiosity and challenge. "Another pawn in the Gagliardi family's game?"

Before I could respond, Carlo intervened, his voice calm but firm. "Silas is under my protection," he said, his gaze steady. "He has no part in our affairs."

Giovanni wasn't satisfied with Carlo's answer. He rose from his seat, towering over me with an intimidating presence. "I don't need your protection," he said, his voice dripping with arrogance. "I can take care of myself."

I felt a surge of anger rise within me, a defiant spark that refused to be extinguished. I may have been only four years old, but I had spent years honing my skills in Karate, Aikido, Tai Chi, Dim Mak, and Qi Gong. I knew how to defend myself, how to harness my internal energy, and how to manipulate it to my advantage.

Without a word, Giovanni lunged towards me, his fists clenched in aggression. Instinctively, I stepped back, evading his attack with the fluid grace of Tai Chi. As he stumbled forward, off balance and vulnerable, I seized the opportunity, striking with precision at his vital points with Dim Mak's deadly efficiency.

Giovanni recoiled, his face contorting in pain as he staggered backwards. I could see the shock and disbelief in his eyes—the realisation that he had underestimated me. In that moment, I felt a surge of power, a sense of triumph that transcended my years.

Even as I stood victorious, I knew that this was only the beginning. The mafia's world was a dangerous place, filled with challenges and adversaries at every turn. And yet, I was ready. I was prepared to embrace my destiny and carve out my own path in the shadow of giants.

As the room fell into stunned silence, I met Carlo's gaze across the table. There was a flicker of pride in his eyes—a silent acknowledgement of my newfound strength. And in that moment, I knew that, no matter what the future held, I would face it head-on with courage and determination. I could tell that the other family was also embarrassed. On the other hand, they felt compelled to conceal the fact that the twelve-year-old's defeat against me didn't yield any profit for them.

The stunned silence that followed Giovanni Montini's defeat hung heavy in the air. Carlo, ever the composed leader, broke the tension by smoothly continuing the business discussions.

"As I was saying," Carlo resumed, his voice steady and commanding, "our proposal involves a collaboration that would benefit both our families." He clearly outlined the terms of the agreement, outlining the mutual benefits of an alliance between the Gagliardi and Montini families.

Across the table, Giovanni Montini's father, Don Vincenzo Montini, was visibly shaken by the events that had just transpired. His face was a mask of conflicted emotions—anger, embarrassment, and concern for his son's well-being. Don Vincenzo was a seasoned patriarch, known for his shrewdness and pragmatism, but in that moment, he was at a loss for words.

Carlo continued to present the terms of the agreement, emphasising the strategic advantages and financial gains for both families. He spoke with authority and confidence, reaffirming the Gagliardi family's commitment to the proposed partnership.

Meanwhile, the Montini family members exchanged worried glances among themselves. It was clear that the incident involving Giovanni had cast a shadow over the negotiations. Their family's pride had been wounded, and they knew that their reputation would suffer as a result.

After a tense few minutes, Don Vincenzo finally spoke up, his voice tight with controlled anger. "We accept your proposal," he said, his words clipped and precise. "Our alliance will be beneficial to both our families."

Carlo nodded, acknowledging the acceptance. "Excellent," he replied, his tone businesslike. "We will finalise the details and move forward with the necessary arrangements."

As the meeting drew to a close, the Montini family members quietly gathered their belongings. Giovanni, still nursing his wounds—both physical and emotional—was led away by his father and other family members. There was an air of shame and disappointment surrounding them, a stark contrast to the confidence they had exhibited earlier.

I watched them leave, feeling a mix of emotions. Knowing that my actions had consequences, not just for Giovanni and the Montini family but for the delicate balance of power in the criminal underworld. Yet he also felt a sense of pride in his abilities, a newfound confidence that he could hold his own in this world of ruthless ambition.

As the Montini family exited the room, Carlo turned to me with a knowing look. "You handled yourself well," he said quietly, his voice carrying a hint of pride. "But remember, strength isn't just about physical prowess. It's about knowing when to act and when to hold back."

I nodded silently, absorbing Carlo's words. Firstly, having spent years understanding that power in the mafia world was a delicate balance of strength, cunning, and restraint, I knew going forward that I would need to navigate this world with caution and intelligence.

The meeting concluded with a sense of cautious optimism. The alliance between the Gagliardi and Montini families had been forged, despite the unexpected turn of events. As I left the room with Carlo, he felt a weight of responsibility settling on his young shoulders. He knew that this was only the beginning of his journey in the dangerous and complex world of the mafia.

But for now, he allowed himself a small smile of satisfaction. This day had demonstrated my abilities not only as the heir to the Gagliardi family, but also as a formidable individual. The event itself would be remembered forever; it both got others to fear me but also taught them that relaxing for physical benefits wasn't helpful at all.

Chapter 5

Days later, it was the date of my birthday. I would follow my usual routine, arriving home at eight p.m. Just half an hour later, the doors would get opened again. My father was there.

We hadn't talked for three months, which was the amount of time since he had been away for business trips again. You should have seen the pleasure in his eyes as he walked straight towards me. His steps intimidated me, causing me to start backing up. I was right. They were not looking forward to seeing me again. He was both drunk and angry. At that moment, I couldn't pinpoint the reason, but it was evident that their emotions clashed.

"Father, I..." I started to explain myself, unsure of what he was upset about, but before I could continue, the first blow landed in my face. This was the first time my own father had beaten me, and to make matters worse, I did nothing to stop it.

"How do you dare to make yourself recognisable? "Another slap and a headache were present for me.

"I..." he interrupted, refusing to allow me to continue. As I attempted to speak, the typically compassionate man turned into a monster, striking me once, twice, and a third time, ensuring that I would remember it not just for the next few days but for weeks.

"Do you know what kind of struggle you could have led us both into?" He wasn't waiting for an answer or any other type of response. He pinned me with each of his arms barely against the wall and looked me deep in the eyes. I didn't cry, sob, or show any other emotions. I was waiting for this to be finished, well aware that I may have been able to fight a twelve-year-old some weeks ago, but it wouldn't be smart to try to do the same against my father, a well-trained mafia soldier.

"Jake, look at me." His harsh way of saying my other name made me react immediately. His jaw was tensed, and his eyes didn't relax on my arms either.

"We are nothing for them. If they desire another one, they will discard us before we even have a chance to look. Yes, the don has paid for your private lessons, but he has enough money to provide the same services to every child on the planet. You are just available right now for him, but if you act like that, he will soon find another one." My eyes hadn't left his while he had been saying each word clearly and honestly towards me. He might have been partially correct, but that didn't encompass his understanding of my previous year's weekly shooting lessons and his consistent support for me.

"Good," I said, and his hands left my arms as he stepped back in shock at his own son's words.

"Good? Nothing is good," he said, and a soft smile of power slowly crossed my face.

"It is good that you don't know everything, while I can have anybody beside me whose month you aren't present." I turned around and left my room, showing him the cold shoulder once I was finished. He didn't come after me this evening. I didn't see him the next morning before I left for training.

At once, Jarle saw me, and his eyes widened in shock. I didn't know how it looked; I hadn't had the courage to look into the mirror that morning to see my failure, at least in my father's eyes.

"Silas, what happened to your face?" Jarle asked, his voice filling with genuine worry as he approached his young student.

I touched the bruise on my cheek with a slight wince. "Ah, I had a confrontation with my father yesterday," I replied quietly. "Things got a bit heated."

Jarle's brow furrowed as he studied me intently. "I see," he said, his tone softening. "I'm sorry to hear that, Silas. Are you alright?"

"Yeah, I'm fine." I reassured him with a nod, trying to muster a smile. "It's nothing I can't handle."

Jarle nodded slowly, his eyes scanning my face for any signs of a deeper injury. Satisfied that I was physically okay, he gestured towards the training mats. "Alright then, let's warm up. We'll start with some light stretching to get your muscles ready."

I followed Jarle's lead, the familiar routine of stretching helping to clear my mind and focus on the training ahead. As we moved through the warm-up exercises, Jarle began to explain the focus of today's session.

"Today, we'll work on refining your karate techniques," Jarle said, his voice calm and reassuring. "We'll start with the basics—stance, strikes, and blocks. It's important to build a strong foundation."

I nodded, feeling a sense of determination wash over me. Despite the turmoil with my father, I knew that training was a place where I could find peace and purpose.

We moved on to practicing Qi Gong—basic techniques such as punches, kicks, and blocks. Jarle watched closely, offering guidance and corrections as needed. With each repetition, I focused on channelling my energy and improving my form.

As the training session continued, the initial stiffness in my muscles gave way to a fluidity of movement. I could feel myself becoming more cantered, more in control of both my body and my emotions.

"Good, sir," Jarle said, nodding in approval. "Your punches are getting stronger, and your stance is more stable. Remember to breathe and stay focused."

I nodded in response, absorbing Jarle's advice. With each strike and block, I found myself pushing aside the distractions and frustrations of the previous day. Training was my sanctuary, a place where I could leave behind the complexities of my family's business and focus solely on self-improvement.

As the session drew to a close, Jarle approached me with a reassuring smile. "You did well today, Silas," he said, his voice filled with pride, while my face continued to inch. Afterwards, I would receive the same question from Steve, as we went further with math and my Spanish learning today. Both of them were obviously worried about me, and later I would see why. My face wasn't only red but also purple and yellow-shaped. I had to take a deep breath, shocked by my own look. I had attempted to suppress the thought, but as soon as I saw it, I realised it was no longer possible.

When I arrived home that evening, I became aware as I approached the house that something had happened. Two black cars, the type that only the most powerful people in our family drove, stood right in front of the house. I stopped as a shiver ran through my spine. What had I done?
I began to sprint towards the house, my mind searching for the words my father had spoken. Had he been right with that, it would have had consequences that I couldn't have foreseen.

At once, as I came closer, I heard familiar voices. The voices were coming from upstairs, so I cautiously entered the building and approached slowly to understand what they were about.

"My don, he is here," I heard an unfamiliar voice say while Carlo and my father left my room. My eyes widened a little while I continued to go upstairs, not wanting to be seen as a listener.

"You are going to come with us." It was the voice of a don, and nobody would reject it. Even as I looked between them, trying to figure out what was happening, my father stepped in front of Carlo to stop him, and with that, we were leaving.

"It was a mistake. I wasn't using my full senses. You have to understand," he said while showing his full height and trying to represent something he usually wasn't.
"You have to be glad that I spared your life. Harming anyone in the family is a reason for release; the fact that it's your own son doesn't give you any further rights. Carlo's voice was cool as he passed him and walked downstairs with me towards his car. My father hurried behind us.

"Jake, you cannot just leave with him. Remember what I told you? "He made a threat, but I remained silent. It would be a lie to say that I wasn't affected at all. I would swallow deeply, unsure what kind of affection my primary action would have for my future. "Sandey, we will see you tomorrow." Before the doors closed, I heard someone say, "Until then, consider your later actions," and I saw my father for the last time in a long while.

That evening, they would check me through to see if it had hurt anything else other than the visible hematomas. Luckily, I was fine elsewhere. The following day, I would not be attending my training or education, but rather attending a meeting with the most significant individuals in my life. Then, my father and both of my teachers will discuss what we are going to do moving forward.

I would sit beside Jarle and Steve, while my father was on the other side and Carlo was to my right on the end of the table. The situation didn't feel right. It would hold my entire future. All my choices now are going to affect the person I will become one day.

Carlo's expression was stern as he addressed my father. "Sandey, you know the rules of our family," he said, his voice steady but firm. "Violence against another member is strictly forbidden."

My father's eyes were downcast, his face a mixture of regret and shame. "I know, Carlo," he replied, his voice barely above a whisper. "I lost control, and I deeply regret my actions."

Steve, my school teacher, spoke up with concern in his voice. "Silas is a bright student," he said, his tone gentle but worried. "He shouldn't be involved in this."

Carlo nodded, acknowledging the gravity of the situation. "Silas," he said directly, his gaze piercing. "You're young, and you have potential, but we can't ignore what happened. It goes against everything we stand for."

I nodded silently, feeling a knot tighten in my stomach. I knew the rules of the mafia family by now, and I understood the severity of my father's actions. On the other side, I couldn't imagine that they would separate us forever.

Jarle, my martial arts instructor, placed a comforting hand on my shoulder. "Silas is a disciplined student," he said, his voice steady and supportive. "He has a lot of potential, which he shows in several ways all the time. However, if his physical condition isn't allowing it,..."

Carlo sighed, his gaze shifting between us. "Given the circumstances," he said finally, "Silas will stay with me for the next six months. We'll reassess the situation after that, depending on Sandey's condition."

My heart sank at the thought of leaving my home, even temporarily, but I knew there was no other choice. I looked at Carlo, silently grateful for his fairness and understanding.

Carlo turned to me, his expression softening. "Silas, I know this is difficult," he said, his voice gentler than usual. "But this is for your safety and your future. You'll continue to study and train with Jarle and Steve as usual."

I nodded, feeling a mixture of apprehension and determination. "Yes, Carlo," I replied quietly.

Sandey placed a hand on my shoulder, his eyes filling with remorse. "I'm sorry, Silas," he said, his voice hoarse. "I promise to make things right."

I nodded, knowing that my father was genuinely remorseful. "I know, Dad," I said softly.

Carlo stood up, signalling the end of the meeting. "Let's give Silas some time to pack the rest," he said, his voice authoritative yet compassionate. "We'll take care of everything else."

As I left the meeting room with Carlo, leaving behind my father and teachers, I couldn't help but feel a sense of unease and uncertainty. But deep down, I knew that Carlo was right. This was a critical time for me—a time to learn and grow, both as a member of the mafia family and as a young man.

As we walked towards Carlo's residence, I silently vowed to make the most of this opportunity, to prove myself worthy of the trust and support that Carlo and my teachers had shown me.

As we stepped inside Carlo's grand residence, the atmosphere changed dramatically. The house was a blend of old-world elegance and modern luxury, with high ceilings, polished marble floors, and opulent chandeliers casting a warm glow throughout the spacious rooms. Rich mahogany furniture and intricate tapestries adorned the walls, exuding a sense of history and power.

Carlo led me through the expansive foyer, past a grand staircase that spiralled upward, its banister gleaming in the soft light. The scent of polished wood and fresh flowers filled the air, creating an inviting, albeit intimidating, environment.

We entered a cosy study, a stark contrast to the rest of the house. The room was lined with bookshelves crammed with leather-bound volumes and framed photographs. A large oak desk stood at the centre, cluttered with papers and personal mementos. Carlo gestured for me to sit in a plush armchair by the window, where sunlight streamed in, illuminating the dust motes that danced in the air.

"Welcome, Silas," Carlo said, his voice softer now. "This will be your home for the next six months, so I would recommend making yourself comfortable." I smiled tightly at him while our eyes met. It was a mixture between a challenge of fire and flame with his coldness, but also a silent promise beneath.

"Thank you; it means a lot to me." My words almost shocked him. People didn't usually say "thanks" to a mafia boss. He might have been accustomed to receiving curses and fighting, but one simple sentence momentarily silenced him.

"Your room will be next to mine. If anything isn't alright," he didn't finish the sentence, as he would never get to the ground for letting me feel good. Additionally, everything had been said without that too. There was no necessity to compose a novel out of that; he merely desired that I perform at the highest level possible and refrain from causing him any distress.

My new routine was adapted to everyday life within a week. It was easy to adjust to living in luxury. Once I became hungry, my breakfast, or any other meal, would simply appear. His writing truly had a deep understanding of me, or perhaps it was simply a reflection of the fact that I wasn't "home" very often. Everything I had done outside of home remained the same. This essentially implied that the sole deviation would be the path I took in the morning and evening. Sometimes I would look toward my old house, wondering if dad was home or if he still thought of me. In the end, half a year was a long time for a four-year-old.

At least it seemed like that in the beginning, but everybody made it as easy as they could for me. After two weeks, my father and I would see him again, which was a very short amount of time compared to the months in which I had been living almost alone before.

We would talk, but mostly I would let them speak. Never had I seen Carlo talking that much and my father laughing so often. It was the first time I had to remind myself that they had once been friends, as my father had been saved by his family. Or at the very least, as long as you have a friend in such a mafia constellation, their power and connections will always play a significant role.

"You don't miss home a lot, do you?" my father asked as I finished my meal, which was compared to what we would prepare for us at home, a five-star-luxury satisfaction. On the other side, this wasn't just about money; it was about me. About something that I had been very bad at sorting out before—feelings. Did I like to be at Carlo's place, or did I miss home?
"Maybe not the house, but your stories would be a miss," I explained while Carlo looked at my father in disbelief.

"What are you telling the kid, love stories?" he said in irony while my father shrugged. It might not be the kindest thing for me to say right now. Not that it made him week, but my father never liked to explain himself for why he did various kinds of acting.

"More about everything, from how I came to be a part of the family to what and who I had been before, but also from work now. At least that was what my last story was about," he explained while rubbing his neck like he almost didn't remember it, since it had been such a long time since then. Carlo would no longer comment on it; he was not one to waste words, and who could argue against a father telling his son goodnight stories?

I would, after this meeting, not see my father again for almost four months. We quickly determined the precise date for the new negotiation.
This day, I would return home to find two intensely focused men engaged in a discussion about a particular theme, which abruptly ceased as soon as I entered the room.

"Hi Jake," my father would say with a tight smile, while Carlo just looked at him, maybe in wonder about the name, which he didn't choose to ask for anyway.

"Hello dad, it's been a long time since we last saw each other," I would say as I walked to my seat on the opposite side of him, facing each other, while Carlo sat beside each of us.

"Yes, it had been a very challenging work trip," he said, and Carlo immediately praised him for mastering it well. Perhaps I was considered "too young" at that time to understand it; spoiler alert: later, they wouldn't stop their conversations as I entered the room.

They continued to talk about something else while I ate my meal, but in the end, the don had an idea. It's almost a rule that you always have to at least consider them, if not act alike, at once.

"Why don't you just move here, Sandey? It would make a lot of things easier." My father's eyes widened for a second, as this wasn't an idea he had considered before, and I am sure that mine is the same.

"Sure, if that doesn't make any sense," he said after a few seconds, while the don smiled more than usual, letting me know that there were several thoughts behind this suggestion. At once, I wondered what this would turn out to be.

Chapter 6

"We are going to take a flight to Italy tomorrow. See it as a birthday present," the don said to me as I went downstairs early in the morning, before my training would start.

I was accustomed to receiving surprises, but I had never received one specifically for me, leading me to question if there was truly no other business connection involved. This is who I would spend the entire rest of the day with, while having to say goodbye to Jarle and Steve for who knows how long. At that time, I believed that a normal visit would last for months, given that my father had always been this far away from home.

The next day I stepped off the plane in Palermo, alongside Carlo, who had been the only one accompanying me. Maybe it wasn't a business trip in the end? My father had been away for half a month already, so he probably wouldn't even recognise our abstinence at home.

The air was warm and fragrant, with the scent of blooming flowers and distant sea breezes. Carlo had decided it was time for me to learn about the roots of our organisation and the very origins of the mafia, and there was no better place than Sicily, the birthplace of Cosa Nostra.

Our first stop was a small village nestled in the Sicilian hills. It was a place where the old ways still thrived, where honour, loyalty, and family values were paramount. As we walked through the narrow, cobblestone streets, Carlo spoke quietly, sharing the significance of this place.

"Silas, this village is where it all began," Carlo said, his voice reverent. "The concept of 'omertà,' the code of silence, was born here. It was a way for families to protect themselves and each other from outside threats."

We visited an old church, its walls lined with frescoes depicting saints and martyrs. Carlo explained how the mafia had intertwined itself with the community, providing protection and enforcing its own code of justice. "The church was often complicit," Carlo said, his tone neutral. "They offered sanctuary, and in return, the mafia supported the local clergy."

In the village square, we met with Don Giuseppe, an elderly man with a weathered face and piercing eyes. He was a living relic of the old ways, having served as an advisor to the local mafia for decades.

Carlo introduced us, and we were invited to sit in the shade of a large olive tree.

"Respect and honour are the foundations of our society," Don Giuseppe began, his voice slow and deliberate. "Every action and every decision must be made with these values in mind. Betrayal is the gravest sin, and loyalty is the greatest virtue."

As Don Giuseppe spoke, I realised the depth of the mafia's roots in Sicilian culture. It was not just about crime; it was about a way of life, a response to the harsh realities of history and survival.

Next, we travelled to Palermo, the bustling capital of Sicily. The city was a stark contrast to the tranquil village. Here, the mafia had evolved, adapting to the complexities of modern life. Carlo and I met a historian who specializes in the mafia's impact on the region.

"The mafia in Palermo is different from the rural mafia," the historian explained. "It's more sophisticated and more integrated with politics and business, but the core values remain the same— family, loyalty, and honour."

We toured the grand Teatro Massimo, where mafiosi once conducted business deals in the elegant opera house's shadows. We saw the Palazzo dei Normanni, where political power had often intersected with mafia influence. Carlo made sure I understood the significance of each place and how the mafia had ingrained itself into the very fabric of Sicilian society.

Throughout our journey, Carlo emphasised the importance of understanding these historical and cultural contexts. "To lead our family," he said, "you must appreciate where we came from and how we've evolved. The lessons of the past will guide our future."

By the time we left Italy, I felt a profound connection to the history and values that had shaped the mafia. The concepts of honour, loyalty, and family were no longer abstract notions but deeply ingrained principles that had guided generations before me. I knew that to respect these values was to honour the legacy of those who had come before us.

As we boarded our flight back home a week later, Carlo looked at me with a mixture of pride and expectation. "Remember what you've learned here, Silas," he said.

"It's not just about power and control. It's about respect, loyalty, and the unbreakable bonds of family."

I nodded, understanding the weight of his words. This journey had been more than an education; it was an initiation into a deeper understanding of my role within our family and the larger legacy we carried forward. Additionally, it was the first time I was away from home. My next problem might be that I would love to do it more often, but I knew that wasn't possible. That was the biggest gift I had ever received—Carlo's time for a week while we also travelled to Italy.

Additionally, he had been teaching me about how people "worked." It made me understand how he would "use" the normal population rather than as a tool for other human beings. The most significant memory for me was when he referred to them as "stupid", "naive", "working tools", or even "scared rats, needing food and sneaking as near they can come, until they run away again, never achieving their goal".

As I had imagined, we would come home to an empty house, and my father would still be on his working trip. We entered the house in silence while the maids hurried upstairs with our baggage. Surprisingly, the don couldn't get enough of the child, with whom he had been on vacation, and struck up a conversation as we made our way to the dining room for a quick meal.

"Name the seven most important points that you learned about the mafia's history on our trip," Carlo asked as he sat down, and I was on my way to the table.

"The importance of Omertà lies in the Code of Silence, which is a fundamental principle in the mafia. It serves as a protective measure for all families and ensures loyalty and trust among the members, while breaking this code is considered the gravest betrayal.

Second, there is the mafia's interconnection with community and religion. Walking through the village and visiting the old church, I saw firsthand how the mafia is woven into the fabric of the community and religion. The church offered sanctuary, and in return, we supported the clergy. This mutual support system showed me that our influence extends beyond crime—it's about being part of the community." Carlo nodded while he listened with a wry smile, and I followed easily.

"The Value of Respect and Honour, for example, as we listened to Don Giuseppe under the olive tree, I understood that respect and honour guide every action. These aren't just words; they're principles that dictate how we interact with others and how we make decisions. Maintaining these values is crucial for preserving the trust and loyalty within our family, which leads us to the next point. The Role of Family and Loyalty. Throughout our journey, you emphasised that family loyalty is everything. Our structure relies on this unbreakable bond. I learned that no matter what, loyalty to the family comes first, and betrayal is the worst sin. This understanding reinforced the importance of our family's unity." Still, no word was being said—just a short nod while I had to continue.

Additionally, I observed the adaptability and evolution of the Mafia. In Palermo, I saw how the mafia has adapted from its rural origins to the complexities of urban life. This adaptability is key to our survival. Learning about our evolution from traditional methods to sophisticated operations taught me that we must always be ready to change and grow with the times. As our family has told me in the past, are we also deeply integrated into political and economic structures. Our meeting with the historian in Palermo further solidified my understanding of this. Our influence extends into politics and legitimate businesses, which helps us maintain power and control. Understanding this integration showed me the importance of being versatile and strategic.

The last one, I would say, is the historical context and cultural heritage. Since the mafia isn't just a criminal organisation, it's a response to historical and social conditions. Knowing this history and heritage helps me better understand our values and operations, and it prepares me to honour and uphold our legacy." Still, after I finished, Carlo remained silent for a moment, simply looking at me and nodding.

"I think I will have to give Steve a salary increase; well done," he said, and I smiled immediately. That was the kindest thing anybody had ever said to me. Throughout the rest of that evening, he would explain to me some changes in my education. For instance, I would follow all the school lessons, but twice a week, I would skip the morning training sessions to continue with my studies. The new subjects are psychology and sociology, history and political science, communication and negotiation, ethics and philosophy, and cultural studies.

Psychology and sociology are essential for understanding human behaviour and social dynamics. Psychology helps in comprehending individual motivations, emotions, and actions, enabling effective leadership and influence over others. It also aids in conflict resolution, persuasion, and maintaining loyalty. Sociology, on the other hand, provides insights into group behaviour, social structures, and cultural norms. This knowledge is crucial for navigating social environments, building networks, and understanding the impact of societal changes on groups and communities.

History and political science offer a deeper understanding of past events and political systems. History provides lessons from the successes and failures of previous leaders and organisations, offering valuable insights into strategies and consequences. Political science aids in understanding political institutions, power dynamics, and governance. This knowledge is vital for strategic planning, anticipating political shifts, and leveraging political connections.

Effective communication and negotiation are critical skills for any leader. Communication ensures the clear articulation of ideas, fostering understanding and cooperation. It is essential for inspiring and guiding teams, managing conflicts, and building relationships. Negotiation skills are crucial for securing favourable deals, resolving disputes, and achieving desired outcomes in various interactions. Mastery of these skills leads to more effective management and influence.

Ethics and philosophy provide a framework for making sound decisions and understanding moral implications. Ethics guide actions and decisions, ensuring they align with moral principles and societal expectations. Philosophy encourages critical thinking, helping to analyse complex situations and consider various perspectives. This grounding fosters responsible leadership and decision-making.

Cultural studies enhance understanding of different cultures, promoting empathy and effective interaction in diverse environments. Knowledge of cultural differences and global historical contexts is vital for building relationships, navigating international scenarios, and adapting to varied cultural expectations. This awareness leads to better communication, collaboration, and strategic planning in a globalised world.

Carlo wouldn't mention a word about the fact that everything had anything to do with the mafia life, but if you think twice, it was exactly what I would need. That hadn't come to mind at the time, but later, as I started to consider all the events he had tasked me with and everything he had "offered," I would see his own interest behind it. I wouldn't hold him accountable for it; ultimately, we all make decisions without much thought, but it could have better equipped me for a future event I now dread.

My father would never get to know about our secret journey. Ironically, he invited me to embark on a secret journey with him immediately after he returned from his work trip. I didn't say anything negative; still, this would never happen. He had been quite enthusiastic when he arrived at the "new" house.

The rest of the year would become harder for me. Not only would I have to study more, but the combination of those who partially shared the home with me would also be a challenge.

Having the two most important people around you doesn't only bring benefits. It also puts you in situations where you must make difficult decisions about who to choose. Yes, you have to make such decisions. They are friends, but still, they have a completely contrasting point of view about the world and want me to educate myself in two totally different ways. I would never have made such choices if I had the option not to; I would prefer to perform twice as much work as necessary to satisfy both, rather than abandoning one of them.

In the end, my days began at six and ended no earlier than eight. At home, I would only eat and sleep. This happens every week, every day. No weekends. No holidays. Time for rest doesn't exist in this world. On the other hand, I utilized my training as a means of relaxation, while the school absorbed 70% of my remaining energy. I loved all the subjects and was really a good student, but still, there was something missing. I'm on the lookout for it, and perhaps I'll discover it in the upcoming year.

Chapter 7

"The event will be in two weeks. Until then, I want you to plan everything precisely. If you plan well, you will receive rewards. However, if you don't…" imagine the most pleasant words you could hear on your birthday from a mafia boss. I nodded hastily and checked out the list he had given me once more to assure myself that it wasn't a dream.

"Plan a family event where everyone is invited for a show while you practice important skills you'll need in the future. Here's a list of how each theme we've talked about relates to planning this event:

1. Leadership and management skills

Basic Leadership: You'll take charge of organising the event. This means making decisions, delegating tasks, and ensuring everything runs smoothly.

Responsibility: You'll be accountable for the success of the event, which means following through on your commitments and making sure everyone knows what they need to do.

2. Strategic thinking and planning

Problem-Solving: Unexpected challenges, such as a performer's last-minute cancellation or a technical issue, may arise. You'll need to think quickly and come up with solutions.

Planning is critical, from choosing a date to deciding on the schedule and ensuring everyone knows their roles. You'll create a detailed plan and timeline for the event.

3. Negotiation and diplomacy

Negotiation Techniques: You may need to negotiate with vendors for the best price on supplies or with family members for their participation and assistance.

Conflict Resolution: If disagreements arise among the planning team or performers, you'll use your conflict resolution skills to mediate and find a solution that works for everyone.

4. Financial Acumen

Money Management: You'll manage the budget for the event, deciding how much to spend on different aspects like decorations, food, and entertainment.

Budgeting: Create a detailed budget plan to ensure you don't overspend and have enough funds for everything you need.

5. Legal Knowledge

Understanding Rules: Ensure that the event complies with any local regulations, such as noise ordinances or public gathering permits. Understanding these rules will keep the event lawful and safe.

6. Security and counter-surveillance

Be aware of the venue and identify any potential safety issues. Ensure there are clear paths for emergency exits and basic security measures in place.

Privacy: Keep guest information private, since not all of the family will be invited. Make sure personal data, like addresses, is secure.

7. Communication Skills

Effective Communication: You'll need to communicate clearly with everyone involved in the event, from performers to guests. This includes giving clear instructions and ensuring everyone understands their roles.

Listening Skills: Actively listen to others' ideas and concerns to ensure that everyone feels heard and valued. This will help in creating a collaborative environment.

By applying these skills to planning the family event, you'll not only ensure its success but also strengthen your abilities in leadership, strategic thinking, negotiation, financial management, legal understanding, security, and communication. This experience will be a valuable step in your personal development and future responsibilities."

I stood in the kitchen, a notepad in hand, ready to plan the family event. Carlo, the Don, had given me the responsibility of organizing a show to entertain a very important guest: Vincenzo "Vince" Romano, a famous singer and an old family ally. His visit was crucial for strengthening our ties with his influential network. This event had to be perfect.

First, I took charge of the overall planning, delegating tasks to different family members. My former caretaker was great with decorations, so I assigned her to transform our backyard into an elegant venue. Jarle had a way with food, so he was in charge of the catering. I knew I had to ensure everyone knew their roles and felt responsible for their parts.

Strategic thinking came into play when I faced some challenges. The sound system we had was outdated and cracked, and I needed a quick solution. I called a few rental places, negotiated a fair price for a high-quality setup, and arranged for its delivery the day before the event. Planning also involved creating a timeline for the evening, from the guests' arrival to Vince's performance and the closing toast by the Don.

My negotiation skills were tested when my former caretaker and Jarle disagreed on where to place the buffet table. I listened to both sides, mediated the conflict, and we agreed on a spot that wouldn't disrupt the flow of guests.

Managing the budget was another task. The Don had given me a set amount, and I tracked every expense, ensuring we stayed within limits. I allocated funds for decorations, food, the sound system, and a small thank-you gift for Vince.

Understanding legal rules was vital. I checked local noise ordinances and ensured our party wouldn't violate any. I also arranged for security, making sure exits were clear and our guests felt safe.

Communication was key throughout the process. I held a meeting with everyone involved, clearly explaining their tasks and listening to their concerns. I also practiced my speech to thank Vince and end the evening after his performance.

The event was a gathering of the most influential members of our mafia family. Among those invited were the key lieutenants who managed different territories, the trusted advisors who counselled the Don on critical matters, and the heads of our various operations, including finance, logistics, and security. Also present were the senior enforcers who ensured our rules were followed, as well as the loyal underbosses who coordinated between the Don and the lower ranks. The event also welcomed a few esteemed allies from allied families, all of whom are crucial to maintaining our power and influence. In total, we had about fifty of our most important figures in attendance.

By the night of the event, everything was in place. The backyard looked stunning, the food smelled delicious, and the sound system worked perfectly. When Vince arrived, he was genuinely impressed. The don gave me a nod of approval, and as Vince sang his first note, I knew all the planning had paid off. It was a night to remember, not just for the entertainment but for the strengthened ties within our family and beyond.

The event was a gathering of the most influential members of our mafia family. Among those invited were the key lieutenants who managed different territories, the trusted advisors who counselled the Don on critical matters, and the heads of our various operations, including finance, logistics, and security. Also present were the senior enforcers who ensured our rules were followed, as well as the loyal underbosses who coordinated between the Don and the lower ranks. The event also welcomed a few esteemed allies from allied families, all of whom are crucial to maintaining our power and influence by impressing them with our event. In total, we had about fifty of our most important figures in attendance.

The event's evening arrived, and our backyard had transformed into a scene of elegance and sophistication. Fairy lights twinkled above, casting a warm glow over the beautifully decorated tables. The air was filled with the aroma of Jarle's culinary masterpieces, and the soft murmur of conversation created a vibrant yet intimate atmosphere.

As the key lieutenants, trusted advisors, and heads of operations mingled, there was an air of anticipation. Vince Romano's presence added a touch of glamour, and his reputation and charisma were evident as he interacted with the guests. The senior enforcers and underbosses, dressed in their finest, maintained a discreet but vigilant watch over the proceedings, ensuring everything went smoothly.

The evening progressed seamlessly. After a sumptuous dinner, the moment everyone was waiting for arrived. Vince took the stage, and as his first notes filled the air, a hush fell over the crowd. His performance was mesmerising, each song resonating with the audience, reinforcing the bonds of loyalty and camaraderie within our family.

Midway through his set, Vince paused and turned to Don, who stood up and addressed the gathering. "Tonight, we not only celebrate our enduring alliances but also the future of our family," he announced. His gaze then settled on me, and I felt a rush of nervous excitement. "Silas, come up to the stage."

Surprised, I made my way through the applauding crowd. Standing next to Vince, under the warm lights, I felt the weight of the moment. Carlo continued, "Silas organised the entire evening. His dedication and leadership have shown he is ready for more responsibilities within our family."

The crowd cheered, and I couldn't help but smile. Vince handed me the microphone, and with a mixture of pride and humility, I thanked everyone for their support. The night had been a success, and now, standing before my family, I felt a deep sense of belonging and purpose. I became unsettled when I observed an individual in the public square, tense and furious, without any other response.

We hadn't informed my father about it, so his emotions could be clearly visible. However, in that moment, I wanted to take advantage of the last seconds of my speech before the obviously upcoming confrontation with him. Carlo nodded at me, reading my thoughts and supporting the idea of making it now rather than at the end of the event. Nobody knew if I had the right to be there. Furthermore, it enhanced my ability to improvise, as this was undoubtedly not a planned event.

"Ladies and gentlemen,

Tonight, as I stand here before you, I am filled with a profound sense of gratitude and honour. Thank you, Don Carlo, for this incredible opportunity and for your kind words. Thank you to all of our esteemed family members and honoured guests for coming here tonight to celebrate with us.

This event is not just about the entertainment and the delicious food we've enjoyed. It's about the strength of our bonds, the loyalty we share, and the legacy we continue to build together. Our family has stood together for generations, navigating challenges and celebrating triumphs as one unified force.

I have learned so much from each of you—leadership, loyalty, integrity, and the importance of family. Each person here has played a pivotal role in shaping who I am today and preparing me for the responsibilities that lie ahead.

Tonight is a testament to the power of our unity. It's a reminder that, as a family, we are stronger together than we are apart. It's a pledge that I take seriously as I move forward in my journey within our family.

As we look to the future, let us continue to honour the traditions and values that have guided us for so long. Let us innovate and adapt to the changing times, never forgetting where we came from or the sacrifices made by those who came before us.

I am deeply humbled to stand here tonight, and I promise to uphold the trust and confidence you have placed in me. Together, we will continue to grow, prosper, and protect our family, our legacy, and our way of life.

Thank you once again for this incredible honour. Let's raise our glasses to our family, our future, and many more successful gatherings like this one. Cheers!"

They all applauded, with my father still standing in the back of the event space, so only we on stage could see him.

At that moment, I was contemplating various forms of punishment simultaneously. No. It wasn't a physical encounter, but rather a two-month-long period of ignorance that clearly demonstrated his disobedience towards my continued involvement in the mafia society. He would converse with Carlo in a normal manner, but it was evident to him that he never said hello or goodbye when I left the school or returned from the training.

The don was the one who made my father start talking to me again on a Friday evening after I had returned from the training. As I entered the room, they would laugh at some sort of joke, and Carlo would ask me to take a seat beside them. I did so, but I didn't meet my father's eyes until I had been there for several minutes. It was tense, but at least he didn't ignore my presence.

"I've planned a trip for the three of us. Whether it's for holidays or further education, there might be some business involved, but the main focus will be on the three of us spending nine days in China. It wasn't my reaction he waited for, since he surely already knew it as soon as the thought of such a trip came to his mind.

A month later, we found ourselves improvising while my father remained silent about his feelings regarding this trip. However, Carlo had planned everything meticulously, from the meetings with our Chinese associates to the sightseeing tours in Beijing and Shanghai. I looked forward to every part of it, eager to explore a new culture and strengthen our family's connections.

During the first few days, we attended meetings and dinners with our business partners. Don Carlo was in his element, negotiating deals and solidifying alliances. I watched him closely, learning how he carried himself with confidence and respect. He was a leader in every sense of the word, and I admired him for it.

In between our business commitments, we explored the wonders of China. The Great Wall took our breath away, and the Forbidden City left us in awe of its grandeur. I noticed my father's demeanour soften as we shared these experiences. He smiled more often and even joined in on conversations about our adventures, or just talked to me at all.

One evening, over dinner in a traditional Beijing restaurant, my father surprised me by asking about my interests and aspirations. It might be rare for such a question to arise, as he had known me for all of his seven years, but it was only then that he actually tried to come closer to his own son. I told him about my interests in sports and my favourite school lessons, and I couldn't stop talking about how much I enjoyed planning the evening with the mafia family. He finally accepted this and stopped blaming me for it.

As the days passed, I felt our relationship grow stronger. We laughed together, shared stories, and even planned future trips as a family. By the time we boarded the plane back home, I knew this trip had brought us closer together. I was grateful to Don Carlo for organizing it, as well as to my father for opening up to me.

China had been not only a journey through a new land, but also a journey towards a deeper understanding and relationship with my father. Back then, I wondered if it would last. The answer to a shift in my future lies in my upcoming meeting with him and Carlo in two weeks. The last one had gone all too fast; to write a book about myself was more challenging than imagined.

Chapter 8

The age of eight is perhaps one of the most beautiful years that can be remembered. The year began with one of the most memorable birthdays, attended by everyone present. Even my father.

I would get an earlier break from my afternoon training session, and as I came outside, a black car waited for me. Together, Carlo and my father Sandey would embark on a road trip to the ocean. As a result, we would take a boat and drive to a restaurant, where we would have one of the best meals I'd ever eaten. Throughout the entire time, the moderator was relaxed; we both laughed and cried out of happiness. At least me. Perhaps it was also my weakest moment.

During the remaining weeks, prior to my father's departure once more, we would go for walks together and engage in conversations that were significantly more frequent than in previous years. He would reach out to my closest friend, opening up and honestly apologizing for his previous years of coldness.

I had always understood it in some way. I used to view myself as a murderer, but in the future, I hope to see myself as a saviour.

As I was usually away from six a.m. to eight p.m. each day, we would sometimes come to my afternoon session and help Jarle teach me even better. They would demonstrate more challenging techniques on each other, which I would then have to try out on one of them.

Sometimes he would also just come to watch us in silence. It somehow felt like a nice gesture, showing me that he at least wanted to make up for the time that had gone by.

The regular monthly meetings proceeded as expected. Some individuals would be "released" from the family, and the methods seemed to become more severe with each passing meeting. They wanted to scare the rest of the family, but I couldn't see the point in doing that while harming their best friend, who had always been trustworthy. Sometimes I wondered if it might make the opposite thing happen. Upon reflection, it appeared as though the number had increased. Previously, we would release two people per year; now, we release the same number of people every month. Also, other factors, such as that we got more interesting for other families or that we had an increasing count of members, could be valid arguments.

One of the ceremonies had an air of gravity that I felt the moment I stepped into the grand hall. The walls were adorned with rich tapestries, and the scent of aged wood and leather filled the air. Don Carlo, our revered leader, stood at the head of the room, his presence commanding respect from everyone present. Next to him was Don Vincenzo, a figure of equal stature and our newest ally, forged from a moment of conflict I had with his son that ultimately proved our family's strength and unity.

I watched all the men, some I had known all my life and others less familiar, file into the room, each taking their place around the long, polished table. There was a hum of anticipation; tonight, we were here to choose new underbosses for the closest parts of our territory. My father, Sandey, stood beside me, his face a mask of indifference. He had never wanted this life, but circumstances had pulled him in, just like a powerful tide sweeps in the unwary. He had made this even clearer to me over the past few days.

The meeting would begin with a few words from Don Carlo. His voice was deep and resonant, cutting through the murmur of the crowd.

"Tonight, we make decisions that will shape the future of our family," he said, his eyes sweeping over each of us. "We have seen the strength of our alliances, and it is time to appoint those who will help us maintain and grow this power."

Don Vincenzo nodded in agreement. His son, who I had bested in a fight that tested more than just our physical abilities, stood behind him, a silent reminder of the trials we had overcome to stand united.

Carlo continued, "We will start by nominating candidates for the position of underboss. This is a role that requires not only strength and loyalty but also wisdom and a deep understanding of our family's values."

Names were proposed, men were discussed, and the merits were debated. My father remained silent, his gaze distant. Despite his reluctance to be involved, he had earned a reputation for his clear-headedness and ability to navigate the murky waters of our family's dealings without losing his moral compass.

As the discussion progressed, it became clear that there was a strong push for my father to be one of the new underbosses. Murmurs of agreement filled the room, and finally, it was Don Vincenzo who voiced what many were thinking.

"Sandey has proven his worth many times over," he said. "He has the respect of our allies and the trust of the family. I nominate him for the position of underboss."

My father's eyes flickered with a mix of emotions, but he remained stoic. The nomination was seconded by several key members, and soon it was time for the vote. One by one, the votes were cast, and it quickly became evident that my father was the overwhelming choice.

Don Carlo turned to him with a solemn expression. "Sandey, you have been chosen by your family. Do you accept this responsibility?"

There was a long pause. My father glanced at me before looking at the faces around the table. He took a deep breath before speaking. "I never sought this position," he began, his voice steady. "I have always tried to avoid the darker sides of our lives—the violence, the pain. However, I understand the importance of this role and the trust that has been placed in me. I will accept this responsibility, but I will continue to do everything in my power to minimise the suffering and loss that comes with it."

A murmur of approval spread through the room. Don Carlo stepped forward and placed a hand on my father's shoulder. On the video, you could see that he was saying something, but it was just me remembering the words exactly.

"Your reluctance is what makes you the right choice, Sandey. It's those who do not seek power who often wield it most wisely. Additionally, think about the amount of time you will have for Silas." They nodded to each other as Carlo turned towards the rest of the family again.

With the formalities complete, the room seemed to relax a bit. Drinks were poured, and the atmosphere became one of celebration. Yet, I could sense the undercurrent of tension that always accompanied such gatherings. Despite the veneer of camaraderie, we all knew the stakes.

This is how the video finished, but I still remember that as the evening wore on, I found myself in a quiet corner, reflecting on the day's events. My father's acceptance of the underboss position was a turning point, not just for him but for our entire family. His presence in this role would bring a different perspective, one that valued life over death and peace over conflict.

Don Carlo approached me, his expression unreadable. "You did well today, Silas," he said. "Your father's reluctance is his greatest strength. He will bring balance to our operations."

I nodded, understanding the weight of his words. "Thank you, Don Carlo. I believe in my father."

Carlo's gaze softened. "And you, Silas, have shown great promise. Your time will come, and when it does, remember the lessons you have learned from your teachers, your father, and me."

As the night continued, I watched my father interact with the other members, his presence commanding a newfound respect. He spoke with Don Vincenzo, who seemed genuinely pleased with the evening's outcome. Their conversation was private, but the smiles and nods suggested mutual respect and shared goals.

The ceremony had been a success, and as the night drew to a close, I felt a sense of pride and anticipation. The future was uncertain, but with my father as an underboss, guided by his principles and supported by powerful allies, I felt confident in the path ahead.

Later, as we prepared to leave, my father turned to me, his expression softer than I had seen in a long time. "Silas," he said quietly, "this life is not easy, and it's not what I wanted for us. But we have to navigate it as best we can. Remember, our strength comes from within, from our ability to make choices that align with our values, even in the face of adversity."

I nodded, absorbing his words. The journey ahead would be challenging, but with my father by my side and the support of Don Carlo and our family, I felt ready to face whatever came next. The ceremony had not just been about choosing new leaders; it had been a reaffirmation of our family's resilience and our commitment to each other.

A month later, the next change would appear. The policy prohibited any underboss from having any beneficial connections to the upper positions. This implied that we needed to relocate.

The house we moved into was just a hundred and fifty meters closer to my school and training centre. The distance from Carlo's villa was the same, but it was longer. Essentially, we would see him on a regular basis. My father would go twice a week to eat dinner with him, while I would join in if I had time, which unfortunately wasn't often.

I never had anybody loosen my daily routine, and it would still last for twelve hours each day. That year also marked the completion of numerous projects. I now speak all the languages I had previously struggled with fluently, like a native speaker. Jarle sometimes shrugged, almost giving up while saying, "I don't know what more I can learn from you," since I was already really good in all of the sports he taught me.

Additionally, I had other classes with Steve. In all of them, I would get straight A's if you translated our system into the most well-known. My private lessons significantly improved my academic performance, allowing me to complete tasks that others would have taken twice as long. On the other hand, I had to go to school every day, sometimes even for ten hours, depending on which day of the week it was and whether I had to quit the two hours of my morning training routine. According to the normal system, I would earn my high school diploma that year. Other lessons and challenges will emerge next year.

However, if we don't skip at once to the end of the year and stay in the time when I moved to the other house with my father, we still have a lot of changes.

My father, now the newly appointed underboss, found his responsibilities multiplying at a pace neither of us had anticipated. The weight of his new role was palpable, bringing with it a series of profound changes.

Sandey had always been a figure of quiet strength in our family, someone who preferred to stay on the periphery of our darker dealings. But as an underboss, he could no longer maintain that distance. His duties expanded rapidly. He was now deeply involved in strategic planning, overseeing operations, and ensuring the smooth execution of our various enterprises. It wasn't just about managing the family's business; it was about steering it through the murky waters of power and politics.

With his new position came longer hours and more frequent absences. Though not for months at a time, the intensity of his work meant that he was often gone from early morning until late at night.

He would leave before dawn broke, and sometimes I would catch only a glimpse of him returning home, his face lined with fatigue but his resolve unwavering. It was a significant shift from the man who used to be more present, even if somewhat reluctantly involved in family affairs.

Yet, along with the increased responsibilities came greater financial rewards. The influx of money was noticeable; our lifestyle, already comfortable, became even more lavish. There were new cars, renovations to our new home, and the best of everything at our disposal. But this wealth, while providing a certain level of comfort, also served as a constant reminder of the price we paid for it.

One evening, I found my father in his study, a rare moment of quiet amidst the chaos. His eyes, though tired, met mine with a look that conveyed more than words ever could. He motioned for me to sit, and we shared a silence that was both heavy and understanding.

Finally, he said, "Silas," his voice steady but weary, "this role demands much from me." More than I ever wanted to give. But it also brings us power and security. I do this for you and the family's future. Remember that."

I nodded, feeling the weight of his sacrifice. "I understand, Dad. I'll do my part too, as always."

In the weeks that followed, I watched as my father navigated his new role with a mixture of determination and resignation. He became a master at balancing the demands placed upon him, all while striving to maintain the moral compass that set him apart. He earned respect not only from his peers but also from me. Despite his reluctance to be part of this life, he carried out his duties with a sense of honour that I aspired to emulate.

Our lives had undeniably changed. The demands on my father were greater and his time more scarce, but the lessons I learned from watching him rise to these challenges were invaluable. He showed me that even in a world fraught with peril and compromise, one could still hold onto their principles and make choices that defined their character.

As I looked towards my own future within the family, I knew that these changes, though difficult, were forging a path that I would one day have to walk, guided by the example my father set every single day.

In the months that followed my father's appointment as underboss, the changes in our lives became the new normal. I watched as he juggled his increased responsibilities, often working late into the night and leaving early in the morning. His absence was felt keenly, but so was the newfound respect and authority he commanded within the family.

Observing him during this time taught me a lot of things. His resilience in the face of relentless demands taught me the value of perseverance. Despite his initial reluctance, he embraced his role with a sense of duty and integrity that set a powerful example. He showed me that true strength lies not just in power but in the ability to remain true to one's principles, even when the path is difficult.

The influx of money and the improvements to our lifestyle were tangible benefits, but they came at a cost. I understood that wealth and power in our world were always balanced by sacrifice and risk. My father's dedication to protecting our family and ensuring our future underscored the importance of loyalty and responsibility.

As I stood on the cusp of my own future within the family, I realised that these lessons were shaping me into the leader I would one day need to become. My father's journey as underboss was more than just a shift in our lives; it was a testament to the strength and resilience that defined the Gagliardi family. It was a legacy I was determined to honour.

Chapter 9

You might have thought that the past few years were challenging, as I had to constantly educate myself and train every day. Compared to my nine-year-old self, these years have been as simple as turning on a light switch.

In the past years, I have learned Karate, Aikido (making other people lose energy), Tai Chi (focusing internal energy and manipulation), Dim Mak (vital points on the body for killing or harming with minimal physics), and Qi Gong (breathing exercises, meditation, and manipulating the body's internal energy) as physical training. We would train them once a week for one theme, so that my qualities wouldn't weaken.

However, I would primarily find encouragement in new fighting sports. My initial experience in boxing and muay Thai enhanced my striking abilities and strengthened my mental resilience.

Since both of them focus on developing powerful and precise striking techniques, these skills are essential for both offensive and defensive situations, allowing a mafia boss to defend themselves or assert dominance when necessary. Additionally, these sports demand a high level of mental resilience. The intense training and sparring sessions build endurance, discipline, and the ability to remain calm under pressure, all of which are crucial qualities for a leader in a high-stakes environment.

I also began learning Brazilian Jiu-Jitsu and wrestling for grappling and control.

They would both teach me effective grappling and submission techniques, which are crucial for controlling an opponent without resorting to lethal force. This control can be vital in situations where physical dominance is required without the intention to kill. These disciplines emphasise leverage and technique over brute strength, providing the ability to subdue larger and stronger opponents. They also teach situational control, enabling me to handle physical confrontations efficiently and effectively.

The last totally new sport was Krav Maga, for practical self-defence and situational awareness. Krav Maga is designed for real-world self-defence. It focuses on neutralising threats quickly and efficiently, using whatever means are necessary. This practicality ensures that I can protect myself in unexpected and dangerous situations. Additionally, it will enhance situational awareness and quick decision-making. These skills are crucial for anticipating and reacting to threats, a necessary attribute for maintaining personal safety and strategic advantage.

I would continue to practice Karate further since it instils a strong sense of discipline and respect, which are essential for leading and managing a criminal organization. The rigorous training and adherence to protocol help in maintaining self-control and authority. It may also be particularly useful for avoiding unnecessary violence while still asserting control.

I wouldn't classify the previous exercise as new either, given that we had already practiced it a little earlier. Strength training will improve overall physical power, endurance, and resilience. A strong physique not only aids in physical confrontations but also commands respect and presence.

If you believe that's all there is, I can assure you that our journey is just beginning. Since I had finished my high school diploma last year, I would also get new subjects at school.

My first new lesson was called Leadership and Management, which covered the fundamentals of effective leadership, including decision-making, team management, and motivational strategies. I would also learn leadership techniques, team-building, and strategic planning.

It would be important for my future, since I must inspire loyalty and command respect from my subordinates. Effective leadership techniques ensure that they can maintain control and motivate my future team.

The second is strategic thinking and planning, which focuses on developing long-term strategies, risk assessment, and contingency planning. In that lesson, I would learn problem-solving, critical thinking, and scenario analysis.

These skills are essential for quick and effective decision-making under pressure. Additionally, it would make me a better analyser of complex situations, and foreseeing potential outcomes is vital for staying ahead of rivals and law enforcement.

My next lesson was maybe the one I liked the least. Financial Acumen. This encompasses financial literacy, budgeting, investment strategies, and comprehending financial markets.

What would make me learn about money management, financial planning, and what my teacher liked most about economic analysis?

I understood the significance of it, and I also achieved the highest grades in that subject. However, my new teacher insisted on calling me "Mr. Harold Fenwick," a name I would continue to use in this and subsequent subjects. However, it's important to note that I have become proficient in efficiently managing funds, a skill that is essential for maintaining operations and enhancing my organisation's influence. It also enhanced my skills in strategic investment, and budgeting decisions have the potential to boost the organization's wealth and stability. I actually didn't dislike all of the above, but Mr. Harold Fenwick would, at least half of the time, teach me to understand financial markets, which helped me make informed decisions about money laundering, investments, and other financial activities.

Ironically, I wasn't too fond of the concept of "legal knowledge." It offers a comprehension of legal systems, business law, and regulatory compliance. It was one of the best subjects for learning legal principles, risk management, and compliance.

Knowing the law helps to avoid unnecessary legal trouble, as does understanding the limits and opportunities within legal frameworks. Risk management was primarily responsible for avoiding such situations. Identifying and mitigating legal risks is critical to protecting the organization from significant setbacks, and ensuring certain operations comply with legal standards can help prevent law enforcement attention and reduce vulnerabilities.

For the next few years, I would be studying security and counter-surveillance. It teaches personal and organisational security measures, surveillance techniques, and counter-surveillance strategies. I acquired knowledge in situational awareness, threat assessment, and security planning.

This might be the subject I enjoyed the most, as I immediately recognised its importance from the outset. Being aware of potential threats and changes in the environment is critical for personal safety and operational security. Identifying and evaluating threats allows for proactive measures to neutralise risks, and in the end, implementing robust security protocols protects the organisation from infiltration, attacks, and law enforcement operations, which we definitely needed.

My last regular school subject was technology and cybersecurity, with the same teacher. The focus was on the latest technological advancements and cybersecurity measures. I acquired knowledge in digital literacy, cybersecurity strategies, and safeguarding data.

Understanding technology is vital for modern operations, including communication, surveillance, and data management. Protecting sensitive information from cyber threats is crucial to maintaining operational integrity and preventing data breaches. In general, good data protection means ensuring the security of digital records and communications to prevent leaks that could jeopardise the organisation.

You might assume that I should calm down and that there hasn't been much change. Other people over the age of nine also have such struggles. Just stop doing that immediately. I wasn't finished with telling you the four new languages I had to learn.

First, Russians have a significant impact on global criminal networks and international business. Understanding Russian could help me navigate and negotiate with my Russian-speaking counterparts.

Additionally, knowledge of the Russian language allows for a deeper understanding of Russian culture and social norms, which can be crucial in forming alliances and understanding rival organizations. Communicating in Russian is critical for covert operations, as is maintaining confidentiality when interacting with Russian-speaking operatives and contacts.

I would also like to learn German, as it boasts the largest economy in Europe. Gaining an understanding of German can lead to numerous legitimate and illegitimate business opportunities, given its widespread usage throughout Europe. It would also be good if increasing my knowledge of the German language helped me understand Germany's complex legal and financial systems, which are important for money laundering and investment strategies.

The next one is Japanese. Since it is a major economic power with significant influence in technology, manufacturing, and finance, speaking Japanese can help in establishing and maintaining business relationships. Furthermore, it may be critical to foster better communication and negotiation when dealing with the Yakuza or other Japanese criminal organizations. Another valid point for this country is that my language skills show respect for Japanese culture and traditions, which can be critical in gaining trust and building strong partnerships.

The last one is Portuguese. Proficiency in Portuguese would assist in gaining access to business opportunities in Brazil and other Portuguese-speaking regions. Portuguese is also spoken in several countries across different continents, including Portugal, Angola, and Mozambique, providing a broad network for potential operations.

Understanding Portuguese culture and language would also assist in integrating with local communities, which is critical for expanding influence and conducting operations smoothly.

As I began to learn all of that, I wished every day that I could have one extra hour instead of twenty-four. My days started at five a.m.

with training, while I had my first classes at seven and wouldn't be finished with learning until six p.m. After that, I would have another training session before finally heading home to grab some food. Luckily, my father would earn enough to employ his own cook, which at least gave me enough time to eat and take a shower before I fell into bed.

The only events I would be part of that year were the monthly family meetings, which nobody dared to skip.

One time, I would encourage a conversation with the guy I once beat up. Giovanni, who was now seventeen, had learned from his mistakes. However, that evening, when our alliance was invited, as we usually do four times a year, we ended up sitting next to each other. At first, he was too shy to even look at me, but later I started to talk to him.

"Hey, Giovanni," I said, trying to break the ice. "How's everything going with you?"

He glanced at me nervously, then looked away. "It's fine," he muttered.

I could sense his discomfort, so I decided to apply some of the psychological techniques I'd been learning. "You know," I said, "I've always found it interesting how people change over time. It seems like you've grown a lot since we last saw each other."

Giovanni hesitated, then nodded. "Yeah, I guess so."

"Do you mind sharing some of your experiences? I mean, what have you been up to lately?" I asked, keeping my tone casual and non-threatening.

He seemed to relax a bit, and after a moment, he started to open up. "Well, after what happened between us, my father made sure I understood the importance of respecting others and not underestimating anyone. I've been focusing a lot on my studies and training."

"That's good to hear," I said, nodding. "What kind of studies?"

"Mostly business and management," he replied. "My father wants me to be well-prepared for when I eventually take over. It's a lot of pressure, but I'm learning to handle it."

I leaned in slightly, showing genuine interest. "That sounds intense. How do you manage to balance everything?"

Giovanni seemed surprised by my interest but pleased to have someone to talk to. "It's not easy. I have a strict schedule. Mornings are for physical training, afternoons for academics, and evenings for learning about the family business."

"Do you enjoy any particular subject?" I asked, steering the conversation towards his interests.

"Actually, I find psychology quite fascinating," he said, warming up to the topic. "Understanding how people think and why they act the way they do is really useful, especially in our line of work."

"Absolutely," I agreed. "It's amazing how much you can influence a situation by understanding people's motivations and behaviours." The irony of hearing that I had inadvertently prompted him to start talking made me almost laugh—a feeling that was as well-hidden as all my other emotions, but I still felt that way.

Giovanni nodded enthusiastically. "Exactly! It's like a game of chess, anticipating moves and strategizing."

"You know," I said. "I've been studying psychology too. It's incredible how it can apply to so many areas of life, including leadership and negotiation."

He looked at me with newfound respect. "Yeah, I didn't realise that you would start at such a young age with something alike. What got you interested in psychology?"

I smiled, recognising the opportunity to keep him talking about himself. "I've always been curious about what makes people tick. But enough about me: What do you find most challenging about your education and training?"

Giovanni thought for a moment. "Probably the expectations. Everyone expects me to be perfect because of who my father is. It can be overwhelming at times."

"I can imagine," I said empathetically. "How do you cope with that pressure?"

"I stay focused by reminding myself why I'm doing this," he replied. "For my family and our future. And, honestly, conversations like this are helpful. It's good to know I'm not the only one facing these challenges."

"You're definitely not alone," I assured him. "We all have our struggles, but it's how we handle them that defines us."

Giovanni smiled, and the tension between us finally dissipated. "Thanks, Silas. I appreciate that."

"No problem," I said, feeling a sense of accomplishment. "We're all in this together, after all."

After that, the conversation flowed more naturally, and I realized how powerful a tool understanding and empathy can be. Giovanni had opened up, not just because I asked the right questions, but also because I showed genuine interest in his experiences. It was a lesson I knew would serve me well in the future. However, at that point, the meeting would suddenly start while I leaned back to listen and analyse everything that would be said. It was a short break for me before everything started over again. I liked the training and schooling, but each day lasting fifteen hours wasn't easy. Luckily, I would get rewarded; if I had known, I would have been looking forward to it. Without this knowledge, I just continued to focus and work to achieve everything with the best grades possible. At that time, I didn't know if it would help me once; now I know that it did, but this is something you are going to learn more about later.

Chapter 10

Two weeks after my birthday, we started a trip, which was a gift for my school performance and a reward for my hard work and dedication. Carlo and my father, Sandey, had planned an incredible journey that would take us to Japan, Portugal, Russia, and Germany. Each country promised new experiences, challenges, and opportunities to use the languages I had been studying so diligently. I was excited, but I also knew that this trip would test my skills in ways I hadn't yet imagined. I only had a year to gain experience from all the countries mentioned above. However, it wasn't just five minutes a day I spent on them; we are speaking of many hours. Therefore, I wasn't negative about my communication skills; I was more certain about how the natives would really talk and if I could understand them.

We began our journey in the land of the rising sun. Japan. As we landed in Tokyo, I felt a mix of excitement and nerves. I had been studying Japanese for months, but now I would have to use it in real-life situations. The bustling city was overwhelming, with its neon lights, towering skyscrapers, and crowds of people.

Carlo had arranged for us to stay in a traditional ryokan, a Japanese inn, to immerse ourselves in the culture. The first challenge came when we arrived at the ryokan. I had to check in using only Japanese.

"こんにちは (Konnichiwa)," I greeted the receptionist. "予約があります (Yoyaku ga arimasu)," I said, meaning we had a reservation.

The receptionist smiled and responded in rapid Japanese. I caught most of it, but I had to ask her to slow down. "もう一度お願いします (Mou ichido onegaishimasu)," I requested. She repeated herself more slowly, and I managed to understand and complete the check-in process.

That evening, we enjoyed a traditional kaiseki meal. The flavours were exquisite, and I did my best to converse with the staff, asking about the dishes and ingredients. Carlo and my father looked on with pride, knowing how hard I had worked to reach this level of proficiency.

One of the highlights of our time in Japan was visiting a dojo, where we watched a karate demonstration. The discipline and precision of the martial artists were inspiring. I even got to participate in a sparring session, putting my own karate training to the test against some skilled opponents. It was a humbling experience, but I held my own and earned their respect.

A few days later, our stay in Japan was already finished, while our travel continued. Our next destination was Portugal. We flew into Lisbon, a city known for its rich history, vibrant culture, and stunning architecture. Portuguese was another language I had been studying, and I was eager to use it.

As we strolled through the streets of Lisbon, I marvelled at the colourful tiles that adorned many buildings. We visited the Jerónimos Monastery and the Belém Tower, each with its own unique charm and historical significance.

One afternoon, we decided to take a tram ride through the city. The trams were a quintessential part of Lisbon's charm, and I enjoyed the ride up and down the hilly streets. At one point, Carlo suggested we stop at a small café for some pastéis de nata, a famous Portuguese pastry.

I approached the counter and placed our order. "Quero três pastéis de nata, por favour (I would like three custard tarts, please)," I said confidently.

The cashier smiled and handed me the pastries. "Muito bem! O seu português é muito bom (Very well! Your Portuguese is very good," he complimented, making me smile for a few seconds before I put the suspected mask on "normal people" again.

We spent our days exploring the city, visiting museums, and enjoying the local cuisine. In the evenings, we would sit by the river, listening to the sounds of fado music drifting through the air. My father and Carlo took this opportunity to teach me more about the history and culture of Portugal, making the experience both educational and enjoyable. While Carlo would bring up the Mafia, my father would roll his eyes and encourage me to explore the other mysterious world, which he had previously lived in and still enjoyed the most.

From Lisbon, we travelled to Moscow. The contrast between the sunny streets of Lisbon and the imposing architecture of Moscow was striking. Russia had always fascinated me, and now I had the chance to experience it firsthand.

Our first stop was Red Square. Standing in the shadow of the Kremlin and St. Basil's Cathedral, I felt the weight of history all around me. I had been learning Russian, and now it was time to use it. It was definitely not the easiest language I have learned, but I would have to try it.

We visited a local market, where I had to negotiate with vendors using my Russian skills. "Сколько это стоит? (Skol'ko eto stoit?)" I inquired, wanting to know the price of a matryoshka doll.

The vendor responded, and I managed to haggle a bit, feeling proud of myself for successfully navigating the transaction. Carlo and my father watched with approval, knowing how important these real-world experiences were for my language development.

While I was unsure about my father's Russian skills, I knew that Carlo could do it perfectly too.

One evening, we attended a performance at the Bolshoi Theatre. The ballet was breathtaking, and even though I couldn't understand every word of the performance, the emotions and beauty of the dance transcended language barriers.

During our stay in Moscow, we also visited a sambo gym. Sambo is a Russian martial art, and I was eager to learn more about it since we had already been discussing it in class. The training was intense, and I had to rely on my physical abilities and the Russian I had learned in order to communicate with my sparring partners. It was a challenging but rewarding experience, and I gained a deeper appreciation for the discipline and skill involved in sambo.

Our final destination was northern Germany, near the Alps. This was a region I had been particularly excited about. The majestic mountains, charming villages, and rich history made it a perfect end to our journey.

We stayed in a small town nestled in the Alps' foothills. The scenery was breathtaking, with snow-capped peaks and lush green valleys. The air was crisp and fresh, a welcome change from the bustling cities we had visited.

German was another language I had been studying, and I was eager to use it. One day, we decided to take a hike in the mountains. We stopped at a small inn along the way to rest and have lunch.

I approached the innkeeper and placed an order for us. "Wir hätten gerne drei Portionen Schweinshaxe, bitte (We would like three portions of pork knuckle, please)," I said.

The innkeeper smiled and nodded, pleased with my effort. "Natürlich! Ihr Deutsch ist sehr gut (of course! Your German is very good," he said.

As we ate, we talked about our journey and the things we had learned. My father, who had been initially hesitant about the trip, seemed to be enjoying himself. Carlo, as always, was a steady presence, guiding us and making sure everything went smoothly.

The highlight of our time in Germany was visiting Neuschwanstein Castle. The fairy-tale castle, perched high on a hill, was even more stunning in person than in pictures. As we toured the castle, I listened to the guide's explanations in German, translating for my father when needed, while Carlo challenged me with picking up some hard words and asking if I knew them.

On our last evening in Germany, we sat by a lake, watching the sun set behind the mountains. It was a peaceful moment, and I felt a sense of accomplishment and gratitude. This trip had been more than just a reward for my school performance; it had been an opportunity to grow, to challenge myself, and to create lasting memories with Carlo and my father.

Looking back on our multi-country adventure, I realized how much I had grown over the course of the trip. Each country had presented its own unique challenges and opportunities, and I had learned valuable lessons along the way.

In Japan, I learned the importance of cultural immersion and respect. Staying in a traditional ryokan and participating in local customs gave me a deeper appreciation for the Japanese way of life. My ability to communicate in Japanese had improved significantly, and I felt more confident in my language skills.

Portugal had taught me the value of exploring new places and embracing different cultures. The vibrant streets of Lisbon, the delicious food, and the warm hospitality of the people had made a lasting impression on me. I had enjoyed using my Portuguese to navigate the city and interact with locals, as well as gain a better understanding of the country's history and traditions.

In Russia, I was challenged by the complexity of the language and the intensity of the culture. The imposing architecture of Moscow, the rich history, and the discipline of the sambo gym had pushed me out of my comfort zone. But I had risen to the challenge, using my Russian skills to navigate the market and communicate with my sparring partners. It had been a tough but rewarding experience.

Northern Germany had been a beautiful and peaceful end to our journey. The majestic Alps, the charming villages, and the warm hospitality of the people made it my favourite part of the trip. I had enjoyed using my German to order food, communicate with locals, and tour the stunning Neuschwanstein Castle. The fresh mountain air and the stunning scenery provided a perfect backdrop for reflecting on our journey.

Most importantly, this trip had brought me closer to Carlo and my father. We had shared new experiences, faced challenges together, and created lasting memories. My father, who had initially been hesitant about the trip, had opened up and seemed to enjoy himself. Carlo had been a steady presence, guiding us and making sure everything went smoothly.

As we returned home, I felt a sense of accomplishment and gratitude. This trip had been more than just a reward for my school performance; it had been an opportunity to grow, to challenge myself, and to create lasting memories with Carlo and my father. I was aware of the lessons I had acquired.

It took months before I could talk to Carlo again. The rest of the time was spent studying and training more of what I had started last year. That day, I returned home a little earlier than usual because Jarle had an appointment later in the evening. Whose hours did I take to go home to Carlo, since my father had been on a working trip for a few days anyway?

As I walked into Carlo's study, I felt a mix of anticipation and nerves. He looked up from his desk, a warm but surprised smile spreading across his face.

"Silas, it's been a while. Come in, sit down," Carlo said, motioning to the chair across from him.

"Thank you, Don Carlo," I replied, taking the seat. "I hope I'm not disturbing you."

"Not at all," he assured me. "It's good to see you. How have you been?"

"I've been busy with studies and training," I said, leaning back in the chair. "There's so much to learn, and I want to be ready for whatever comes next."

Carlo nodded with a thoughtful expression. "You're doing well, Silas. Your dedication is admirable. But remember, it's important to find balance. All work and no rest can wear anyone down."

"I know," I admitted. "That's partly why I wanted to talk to you. I've been thinking a lot about our trip and everything I learned. It made me realise how much more there is to understand."

"I'm glad to hear that," Carlo said. "What specifically has been on your mind?"

"I've been reflecting on the different cultures we experienced," I began. "Japan, Portugal, Russia, and Germany each had their own unique way of life, values, and traditions. It made me realise how interconnected the world is and how important it is to understand these differences."

"That's a valuable insight," Carlo agreed. "In our line of work, understanding cultural nuances can make a significant difference. It can help in negotiations, building alliances, and even avoiding conflicts."

"Exactly," I said, feeling encouraged. "But I also realised how much more I needed to improve my language skills and cultural knowledge. Each encounter taught me something new, but it also showed me my limitations."

"Improvement is a continuous process," Carlo said, leaning forward. "Even I am always learning. The key is to remain open and curious. You're already on the right track if you recognize what you need to work on."

"I appreciate that, Carlo," I said sincerely. "Another thing that stood out to me was the importance of leadership. Watching you and the way you handle situations—it's something I aspire to."

Carlo's gaze intensified. "Leadership is crucial, Silas, and it's something that can't be learned solely from books. You need practical experience. Your studies are important, but so is being in the field, understanding the dynamics of our operations firsthand."

"I understand," I said, a little unsure. "What do you suggest?"

"I want you to spend more time with me and the other leaders," Carlo said. "Join our meetings; observe how decisions are made and how negotiations are handled. It's time you start understanding the practical side of things."

I nodded, feeling a mix of excitement and apprehension. "I'd like that, Carlo." I want to learn everything I can."

"Good," he said. "We'll start as soon as possible. While we acknowledge that you still need to focus on your studies, I believe your father would not be pleased to learn that you are spending your time in other activities.

"Yeah, I know." I looked to the ground for a moment, searching for alternatives.

"And Silas," Carlo continued, "I want you to understand that this is about more than just observing. I expect you to participate, ask questions, and share your insights. You're smart and capable, and it's time you start using those skills in real-world scenarios."

"I will," I said, feeling a surge of determination. "I will try to figure out anything. Thank you, Carlo."

"You're welcome," he said. "Remember, this is a step towards your future. The more you learn now, the better prepared you'll be when it's your turn to lead." My eyes widen for a second, and my mouth opens. He had never told me so clearly that this was his purpose with me. Even if I had thoughts about it, it would always just be my imagination about what he might want from me, never any direct words.

As I left Carlo's with a nod and an assurance that I would find any way to get closer to "his world," I felt a renewed sense of purpose. The conversation had given me clarity and direction, reinforcing my commitment to my education and training. But now, I also understand the importance of practical experience—being in the field and learning from real-world situations.

The remaining part of the year passed swiftly. I discussed my ideas with my tutors, who informed me that I had two options: either continue studying the same way and have more time for it next year, or attend some meetings while still facing the same time pressure. I chose the first. It wasn't easy, but I had something to look forward to. Even if I was a bit unsure if it was what I wanted for my later life, not knowing what exactly it involved, Carlo would stand by my side once I started to dwell and support me.

My father would remain unaware of these plans. Our relationship was good, even though we only saw each other in the mornings and at dinner for a little longer. However, neither Carlo nor I could convince him to support my idea. That's why we chose to keep it a secret. Later, it would present me with new challenges, but at the age of ten, it was all I had, and I didn't have much time with either of them.

Chapter 11

As promised, I have completed the most extensive studies from the previous years and will continue to focus on enhancing my language skills while participating in more "practical" activities. The first event took place a week after my birthday, and I was nervous from the moment I learned that I would be participating.

The venue was an elegant Italian villa nestled amidst sprawling vineyards and olive groves. It exuded an air of sophistication and power, much like the men who gathered within its walls. It was my first Mafia meeting, and I couldn't help but feel a mix of excitement and trepidation as I stepped out of the car and followed my father, Sandey, towards the entrance.

Don Carlo, the head of our family, greeted us with a warm smile as we entered. Despite his imposing presence, there was a kindness in his eyes that put me at ease. He was a mentor to me, someone I looked up to and respected deeply.

The room was filled with men in impeccably tailored suits, their faces familiar yet intimidating. They were our organization's captains, each with their own domain of influence and power. As I scanned the room, I realised the weight of the responsibility that awaited me in the years to come.

Don Carlo motioned for us to take our seats at the long, mahogany table that dominated the centre of the room. I sat beside my father, feeling a surge of pride mixed with apprehension. This was the moment I had been preparing for—the first step towards my future in the family business.

The meeting began with a discussion of current affairs, ranging from business dealings to territorial disputes. Don Carlo presided over the proceedings with calm authority, listening intently to each speaker before offering his own insights and guidance.

As the discussions progressed, I found myself drawn into the conversation, eager to contribute despite my lack of experience. I listened intently to the discussions, absorbing every detail and committing it to memory. This was my chance to prove myself and show that I was worthy of my place at the table.

At one point, the topic turned to a recent dispute between two rival families. Tensions were running high, and there was talk of retaliation. Don Carlo listened quietly, his expression unreadable as he weighed the options before him.

Sensing the tension in the room, I spoke up, my voice steady despite the nerves that threatened to betray me. I offered a suggestion—a compromise that would defuse the situation without resorting to violence. It was a risky move, but one that I felt was necessary.

To my surprise, Don Carlo nodded in agreement, acknowledging my contribution with a small smile. It was a small victory, but one that filled me with a sense of pride and accomplishment. In that moment, I knew that I had earned his respect, if only for a fleeting moment.

As the meeting drew to a close, I felt a sense of relief wash over me. I had survived my first Mafia meeting, emerging unscathed and even earning a measure of respect from my peers. It was a small victory, but one that filled me with confidence as I looked towards the future.

In the days that followed, I reflected on the experience, dissecting every word and gesture in search of meaning. I knew that this was just the beginning of my journey in the family business, and that there would be many more challenges and obstacles to overcome.

However, for now, I allowed myself to bask in the glow of my success, knowing that I had taken the first step towards my destiny as a leader in the world of organised crime. With Don Carlo by my side, I knew that anything was possible.

Already two days later, he would inform me that we would have to go to another spontaneous meeting with another Mafia boss.

This boss was known as Don Salvatore, the second most powerful man in the world of organised crime.

The news came as a surprise, and I couldn't help but feel a sense of apprehension at the thought of meeting such a formidable figure. Don Salvatore was renowned for his ruthlessness and cunning, and the prospect of facing him filled me with a mixture of fear and excitement.

As we made our way to the meeting, I couldn't shake the feeling of unease that gnawed at the pit of my stomach. This was uncharted territory for me—a chance to prove myself on a much grander scale than before.

When we arrived at the designated location, a luxurious mansion on the outskirts of town, I was struck by the opulence of the surroundings. It was a stark contrast to the austere elegance of Don Carlo's villa, a testament to Don Salvatore's wealth and power.

We were ushered into a grandiose dining room, where Don Salvatore awaited us at the head of the table. He was a formidable figure, his presence commanding respect and deference from all who were present.

The meeting began with the customary exchange of pleasantries, but it was clear that there was tension simmering beneath the surface. Don Salvatore wasted no time in getting down to business, outlining the purpose of our gathering with steely determination.

As the discussion unfolded, I found myself once again drawn into the fray, offering my insights and suggestions with a newfound confidence. Despite my youth and inexperience, I held my own in the presence of these seasoned veterans of the underworld.

To my surprise, Don Salvatore seemed impressed by my contributions, acknowledging my input with a nod of approval. It was a surreal moment to stand face to face with one of the most powerful men in organized crime and earn his respect, while I often forgot that Carlo was even more powerful than him.

As the meeting drew to a close, I couldn't help but feel a sense of pride at having survived the encounter unscathed. It was a testament to my growing confidence and abilities, a sign that I was beginning to find my place in this world of shadows and secrets.

As we made our way back to Don Carlo's villa, I reflected on the events of the day with a mixture of satisfaction and trepidation. This was just the beginning of my journey into the heart of darkness, and I knew that the road ahead would be fraught with danger and uncertainty.

However, with Don Carlo by my side, I felt ready to face whatever challenges lay ahead. Together, we would navigate the treacherous waters of the underworld, forging alliances and building our empire one step at a time. And with each passing day, I grew more confident in my abilities, knowing that I had the guidance and support of the most powerful man in the world of organised crime.

This pattern continued every week, sometimes even on a daily basis. There were two meetings in a single day, and it became increasingly challenging to conceal them from my father, who lived in the house next to Carlo's villa. However, up until now, he hasn't inquired or mentioned anything about it, likely due to his busy schedule with his group.

One day, Don Carlo summoned me to accompany him on a journey into the depths of the underworld—the black market and underground economy. It was an opportunity to witness firsthand the clandestine dealings and illicit activities that fuelled the shadowy underbelly of our world.

As we ventured into the heart of the city, I couldn't help but feel a mixture of excitement and apprehension. The streets were teeming with life, yet there was an air of danger lurking beneath the surface. Don Carlo led the way with an air of confidence, navigating the maze of alleyways and backstreets with ease.

Our first stop was a dimly lit warehouse on the outskirts of town, where a network of underground traders gathered to exchange goods and services. The atmosphere was tense, filled with whispered conversations and furtive glances as deals were struck in the shadows.

Don Carlo introduced me to some of the key players in the underground economy, each with their own specialties and connections. From smugglers to counterfeiters, the range of illicit activities was staggering, yet there was a sense of camaraderie among those who operated in this world of darkness.

As we moved deeper into the black market, I witnessed transactions taking place in every corner, from illegal weapons to stolen goods and contraband. It was a thriving marketplace of vice and temptation, where anything could be bought for the right price.

One of the more unsettling aspects was the presence of prostitution, with women and men alike offering their services in dark corners and back rooms. It was a stark reminder of the darker side of human nature, where exploitation and desperation intersected. Not that there's anything wrong with the work in general, but whose who did it here under the influence of drugs, hadn't reached a certain legal age, or possibly even worked illegally for someone else.

Despite the allure of the forbidden, I remained vigilant, knowing that one misstep could have dire consequences. Don Carlo watched over me like a guardian angel, guiding me through the treacherous waters of the underworld with a steady hand.

As the day drew to a close, I couldn't help but feel a sense of awe at the sheer scale and complexity of the black market and underground economy. It was a world unto itself, operating in the shadows of society while exerting a powerful influence over the world above.

As we made our way back to the safety of my training centre, Jarle was already waiting for me. I reflected on the day's events with a mixture of fascination and unease. I had glimpsed the dark underbelly of our world, and it had left an indelible mark on my soul.

On the other side, amidst the darkness, I found solace in the knowledge that I had Don Carlo by my side, a beacon of strength and wisdom in a world consumed by chaos and corruption. And as we crossed the threshold into daylight, I knew that I was one step closer to fulfilling my destiny in the world of organized crime.

As promised, I completed the most substantial studies of recent years and now focus solely on refining my language skills while engaging in practical events. The anticipation built from the moment I learned I would be part of these gatherings, and the first one took place just a week after my birthday.

The venue, an elegant Italian villa nestled amidst sprawling vineyards and olive groves, exuded sophistication and power. It was my initiation into the world of the Mafia, and I couldn't help but feel a mix of excitement and trepidation as I entered alongside my father, Sandey.

Don Carlo, the head of our family, greeted us with warmth as we stepped inside. Despite his imposing stature, there was a kindness in his eyes that put me at ease. He was my mentor, someone I admired and respected deeply.

The room was filled with men in impeccably tailored suits, each holding their own domain of influence and power. I scanned the room, realising the weight of the responsibility that awaited me in the years to come.

Don Carlo motioned for us to take our seats at the long, mahogany table that dominated the room. I sat beside my father, feeling a surge of pride mixed with apprehension. This was the moment I had been preparing for—the first step towards my future in the family business.

The meeting commenced with discussions ranging from business dealings to territorial disputes. Don Carlo presided with calm authority, listening intently before offering his insights.

Amidst the discussions, I found myself drawn in, eager to contribute despite my lack of experience. I absorbed every detail, committed to memory, eager to prove myself worthy of my place.

At one point, the discussion turned to a recent dispute between rival families. Sensing the tension, I spoke up, offering a suggestion to defuse the situation. To my surprise, Don Carlo nodded in agreement, acknowledging my contribution with a small smile.

While the meeting concluded, I felt a sense of relief mixed with pride. I had navigated my first Mafia meeting, earning respect from my peers and Don Carlo himself.

However, the challenges continued. Days later, Don Carlo informed me of another meeting, this time with Don Salvatore, the second most powerful man in the world of organised crime.

This encounter posed a new set of challenges and uncertainties. Yet, with Don Carlo's guidance, I ventured into the meeting, facing Don Salvatore with a newfound confidence.

Each meeting brought new lessons and insights, shaping my understanding of the Mafia world. Yet doubts lingered. Did I truly want this life for myself? Was it worth the sacrifices and dangers that followed?

As I continued to attend these meetings, grappling with these questions, my father's stories of a different life on the other side of the world echoed in my mind. The uncertainty of my future weighed heavily on me, leaving me to wonder which path I would ultimately choose.

Days turned into weeks, and I found myself immersed in the world of organised crime. Meetings with other Mafia bosses became a regular occurrence, each one testing my resolve and pushing me to the limits of my capabilities.

One day, Don Carlo summoned me to accompany him on a journey into the depths of the underworld—the black market and underground economy. It was an opportunity to witness firsthand the clandestine dealings and illicit activities that fuelled the shadowy underbelly of our world.

As we ventured into the heart of the city, I couldn't help but feel a mixture of excitement and apprehension. The streets were teeming with life, yet there was an air of danger lurking beneath the surface. Don Carlo led the way with an air of confidence, navigating the maze of alleyways and backstreets with ease.

Our first stop was a dimly lit warehouse on the outskirts of town, where a network of underground traders gathered to exchange goods and services. The atmosphere was tense, filled with whispered conversations and furtive glances as deals were struck in the shadows.

Don Carlo introduced me to some of the key players in the underground economy, each with their own specialties and connections. From smugglers to counterfeiters, the range of illicit activities was staggering, yet there was a sense of camaraderie among those who operated in this world of darkness.

As we moved deeper into the black market, I witnessed transactions taking place in every corner, from illegal weapons to stolen goods and contraband. It was a thriving marketplace of vice and temptation, where anything could be bought for the right price.

One of the more unsettling aspects was the presence of prostitution, with women and men alike offering their services in dark corners and back rooms. It was a stark reminder of the darker side of human nature, where exploitation and desperation intersected.

Despite the allure of the forbidden, I remained vigilant, knowing that one misstep could have dire consequences. Don Carlo watched over me like a guardian angel, guiding me through the treacherous waters of the underworld with a steady hand.

As the day drew to a close, I couldn't help but feel a sense of awe at the sheer scale and complexity of the black market and underground economy. It was a world unto itself, operating in the shadows of society while exerting a powerful influence over the world above.

As we made our way back to the safety of my training centre, I reflected on the day's events with a mixture of fascination and unease. I had glimpsed the dark underbelly of our world, and it had left an indelible mark on my soul.

On the other side, amidst the darkness, I found solace in the knowledge that I had Don Carlo by my side, a beacon of strength and wisdom in a world consumed by chaos and corruption. And as we crossed the threshold into daylight, I knew that I was one step closer to fulfilling my destiny in the world of organized crime.

The months passed, and I continued to attend meetings, each one adding to my knowledge and experience. I began to understand the intricacies of our family's operations, from the logistics of illegal trades to the delicate balance of power and influence.

Yet, as my understanding grew, so did my doubts. The weight of my future in the Mafia hung heavy on my shoulders, and I wondered if this was truly the path I wanted to take. My father's stories of a different life echoed in my mind, reminding me of the possibilities beyond the shadows.

As I grappled with these questions, I sought solace in my studies, burying myself in books and language lessons. The languages of the world became my escape, offering a glimpse into cultures and lands far beyond the reach of organised crime.

And so, as I stood at the crossroads of my destiny, I wondered which path I would ultimately choose. Would I embrace the life laid out before me, with its risks and rewards, or would I forge my own path, away from the shadows and into the light?

The uncertainty about my future lingered, a constant companion as I navigated the complexities of the Mafia world. And as I looked toward the horizon, I knew that the decisions I made would shape not only my destiny but also the future of our family.

Chapter 12

"Happy Birthday," you could have said, but no, a bottle with ice-cold water was the tradition. My twelfth birthday, there it was. Today was the only day which I was anything "special" and the day as mine celebrated. Today marked the beginning of my official work, primarily signifying my status as an official "man" within the community.

I shot up in bed, gasping as the freezing water soaked through my sheets and clothes. My father, Sandey, and Don Carlo stood at the foot of my bed, grinning. It was a tradition I had heard about countless times, but experiencing it firsthand was something entirely different. I couldn't help but laugh through the shivers, knowing this was just the beginning of a long and eventful day.

"Get dressed, boy," my father said, his voice full of pride and a touch of amusement. "Today, you become a man."

I quickly changed into the clothes laid out for me—a finely tailored suit, the best I'd ever worn. I could feel the weight of the fabric and the responsibility it symbolized. As I dressed, I thought about all the lessons and training that had led up to this moment. Today was not just a birthday; it was a rite of passage into a world that demanded loyalty, strength, and cunning.

The day began with a family breakfast, a rare occasion where everyone gathered around the table. My father, Don Carlo, and other key members of our family were there. The atmosphere was filled with a sense of solemnity and celebration. As I sat down, I felt the eyes of the men around me, evaluating, judging, and, in some cases, approving.

"Silas," Don Carlo began, raising his glass, "today, you join us not as a boy, but as a man. You have shown promise, dedication, and loyalty. We are proud to welcome you officially into our world."

I nodded, feeling a mixture of pride and nervousness. The men around the table raised their glasses, and I followed suit. The toast marked the beginning of my new role in the family, one that came with privileges and responsibilities.

After breakfast, the real festivities began. The villa was bustling with activity as preparations for the celebration continued. I was taken to meet various family members and associates, each offering their congratulations and a piece of advice. The air was thick with the scent of flowers, as well as the sound of laughter and music.

By midday, the villa's gardens were filled with guests. Tables were laden with food, and there were games and activities for the children. However, the most significant part of the day was the ceremony that would officially mark my induction.

The ceremony took place in the villa's grand hall, a room steeped in history and tradition. As I stood at the front, surrounded by the family and our closest allies, Don Carlo stepped forward to address the gathering.

"Today, we gather to welcome Silas as an official member of our family. He has proven himself worthy, and it is time for him to take on the responsibilities and privileges that come with his new role."

He turned to me, his gaze intense and unwavering. "Silas, do you swear to uphold the values of our family, to protect our interests, and to remain loyal, no matter the cost?"

"I swear," I replied, my voice steady despite the weight of the moment.

Don Carlo nodded and handed me a small, ornate dagger. "This dagger symbolises your commitment to the family. Keep it with you always, as a reminder of your oath."

I took the dagger, feeling the cold metal against my palm. It was both a weapon and a symbol—a reminder of the path I had chosen.

The ceremony continued with more speeches and toasts, each reinforcing the significance of the day. As the official proceedings came to an end, the atmosphere shifted to one of celebration. Music filled the hall, and guests began to mingle and enjoy the festivities.

Throughout the day, I was introduced to more family members and our associates. Each interaction was a lesson in diplomacy and power dynamics. I gained a deeper understanding of the subtle cues and signals that governed our world, surpassing my previous understanding.

One of the more memorable encounters was with Enzo, a senior member of the family known for his wisdom and experience. He pulled me aside, his eyes twinkling with a mix of amusement and seriousness.

"Silas, today you become a man, but remember, true power lies not in force but in understanding people. Know their desires, their fears, and their motivations, and you will be a step ahead."

I nodded, absorbing his words. It was advice that would serve me well in the years to come.

As the sun began to set, the celebration moved to the villa's gardens, where a grand feast awaited. The tables were filled with an array of dishes, from traditional Italian fare to exotic delicacies. The air was filled with the sound of laughter and clinking glasses as everyone enjoyed the feast.

As I moved through the crowd, I couldn't help but notice the looks I was getting from some of the women present. Being "free" for women was a part of my new status, something I had heard about but never fully understood until now. The attention was both flattering and intimidating, a reminder of the new world I was stepping into.

Among the guests was Cecilia, a girl around my age, known for her sharp wit and striking beauty. We had crossed paths a few times before, since she belonged to our alliance family, but today she seemed different and more approachable. She caught my eye and smiled, a gesture that sent my heart racing.

"Congratulations, Silas," she said, her voice smooth and confident. "It appears you're the star of the show."

"Thank you, Cecilia," I replied, matching her confidence but cooler. "It's a big day for me."

She nodded, her eyes twinkling with curiosity. "So, how does it feel to be an official man in the family?"

"It's overwhelming," I admitted. "But it is also exciting. There's a lot to learn and a lot to be responsible for."

She laughed, a melodious sound that made me tense, knowing that everything I did here would be seen. "You'll do fine, Silas. Just remember to stay true to yourself."

As the night deepened, the atmosphere grew more relaxed yet still charged with energy. The guests danced and mingled, with the music and laughter creating a symphony of celebration. It was a night that seemed to stretch on forever, each moment a reminder of the world I was now a part of.

In the midst of the celebration, Don Carlo approached me, his expression one of pride and approval.

"Silas, you have done well today," he said. "You have shown poise and maturity beyond your years. I have no doubt you will continue to make us proud."

"Thank you, Don Carlo," I replied, feeling a surge of gratitude and determination.

He placed a hand on my shoulder, his grip firm and reassuring. "Remember, you are not alone in this journey. We are family, and we stand together."

As the night drew to a close, I found a moment of solitude in the villa's garden. The air was cool and crisp, a welcome contrast to the warmth and energy of the celebration inside. I took a deep breath, reflecting on the day's events and the path that lay ahead.

My mind wandered to my father, Sandey, who had watched me with pride and a hint of sadness throughout the day. He had never wanted to be part of this world, yet circumstances had pulled him in. I wondered what he thought of my journey and the choices I was making.

Lost in thought, I didn't notice Cecilia approaching again until she was standing beside me. I had to control myself not to roll my eyes at her clinginess.

"Penny for your thoughts?" she asked, her voice soft and teasing.

I made a half-smile and looked at her for a second, almost appreciating the value of this communication. "Just thinking about everything that's happened today, nothing else," I pronounced sharply, in the hope of making her understand that she should stay away.

She nodded with a thoughtful gaze. "It's a big step to becoming a man in the family. But I think you're ready for it."

"Do you really?" I asked, genuinely curious, hoping to find a game in the conversation that better suited me.

"Yes," she replied without hesitation. "I've seen the way you handle yourself and the way you interact with people. You have a natural presence, Silas. People respect you, and they listen to you. That's not something you can learn; it's something you have."

Her words were a comfort, a reassurance that I was on the right path. We stood there in silence for a moment, the night sky stretching above us, a tapestry of stars and possibilities.

As the celebration wound down and guests began to depart, I felt a sense of accomplishment and a deep, abiding uncertainty. The day had been a whirlwind of emotions and experiences, each one a step towards my future in the Mafia.

However, as I lay in bed that night, the weight of my new role pressed heavily on my mind. The world of the Mafia was complex and dangerous, filled with shadows and secrets. And while I had taken my first steps into this world, I couldn't help but wonder if this was truly the life I wanted.

My father's stories of a different life, of choices and paths not taken, echoed in my mind. His journey had been one of struggle and sacrifice, a reminder that the world was vast and filled with possibilities beyond the confines of our family.

The question lingered, unanswered and persistent: Would I continue down this path, embracing the life of power and influence that awaited me, or would I seek a different destiny, one that offered freedom and self-discovery?

After that day, everything changed. Increased responsibilities meant that Carlo would assign tasks for me to complete. I wasn't proud of some of the tasks at first, but I quickly adapted to them. It didn't take long for them to bring me back to the black market, where I secured my first real job—the port.

I had to decide whether ships were coming and where their deliveries should go. The docks were a chaotic hub of activity, with cargo being unloaded and loaded at all hours. It was a place where deals were made in the shadows, and every movement was watched closely. I was given a small office overlooking the harbour, from which I could oversee operations and ensure everything ran smoothly.

My first day at the port was overwhelming. The sheer volume of goods passing through was staggering—everything from legitimate imports to contraband that needed to be moved discreetly. My role was to make sure that the shipments were directed to the right places and people without attracting unwanted attention.

"Keep an eye on the manifests," Carlo had instructed. "Make sure nothing goes where it shouldn't. And remember, you're the eyes and ears here."

It was a significant responsibility, one that required both vigilance and discretion. I quickly learned to read the subtle cues and signals from the dockworkers, understanding which shipments needed special handling and which were routine.

One of my first tasks was overseeing a shipment of illicit weapons destined for a neighbouring family. The crates were marked as agricultural equipment, a common ruse to avoid detection. I watched as the dockworkers unloaded the crates, my heart pounding as I checked the manifest against the actual cargo.

"Is everything in order?" one of the workers asked, his tone casual but his eyes sharp.

I nodded, doing my best to project confidence. "Looks good. Make sure it gets to the warehouse without any delays."

The worker nodded and went back to his task, and I felt a small surge of relief. It was a minor victory, but each successful task built my confidence and my understanding of the operations.

As the days turned into weeks and weeks into months, I became more comfortable in my role. I learned to navigate the complex web of relationships and alliances that governed the black market. I knew who to trust and who to be wary of, and I began to understand the delicate balance of power that kept everything running smoothly.

One night, as I was wrapping up for the day, Carlo came to see me. His presence at the port was rare, and I knew it must be important.

"Silas," he said, his voice low and serious, "there's something I need you to handle personally."

He handed me a file, and I opened it to see details of a shipment of high-value narcotics scheduled to arrive the next morning. The shipment was critical to our operations, and it needed to be handled with the utmost care.

"I trust you to make sure this goes off without a hitch," Carlo said, his gaze intense. "This is important. Don't let me down."

I nodded, feeling the weight of his trust and the responsibility it entailed. The next morning, I was at the port before dawn, overseeing every detail of the operation. The shipment arrived as scheduled, and I watched as the dockworkers carefully unloaded the crates.

Everything was going smoothly until one of the workers signalled that there was an issue with one of the crates. My heart sank as I approached, fearing the worst.

"What's the problem?" I asked, keeping my voice steady.

"The seal is broken," the worker replied, pointing to a crate with a visibly tampered seal. "It might have been compromised."

I felt a surge of panic, but I forced myself to stay calm. I knew that any sign of weakness or uncertainty could be disastrous.

"Check it thoroughly," I ordered. "Make sure everything is accounted for."

The workers pried open the crate and began inspecting the contents. I watched anxiously, my mind racing with possible scenarios. If the shipment was compromised, it could mean serious trouble for us.

After what felt like an eternity, the worker turned to me and nodded. "Everything's here. It looks like the seal was damaged during transport."

While I felt a sense of relief, the incident served as a stark reminder of the constant vigilance required in this line of work. I made a mental note to double-check all shipments in the future, ensuring that nothing slipped through the cracks.

As the months passed, my responsibilities grew, and so did my confidence. I handled shipments of all kinds—drugs, weapons, counterfeit goods—each one teaching me more about the intricate operations of the black market. I built relationships with key players, earning their trust and respect through my competence and reliability. Despite the benefits of starting in a leading position, I found that it required more mental effort than physical exertion. I later realized that Carlo only wanted me to do this so that I could understand how the business operated at each location.

However, with increased responsibilities came increased risks. One evening, as I was closing up the port, I received a call from one of our informants. There was a rumour that the authorities were planning a raid on our next shipment.

I immediately contacted Carlo, who instructed me to move the shipment to a safer location and make sure that none of our men were caught in the raid. It was a tense and dangerous task, requiring quick thinking and careful planning.

In the darkness, I coordinated the shipment's relocation, using trusted men and discreet routes to avoid detection. The operation proceeded smoothly, and upon the arrival of the authorities the following day, they discovered only empty docks.

Carlo was pleased with my handling of the situation, which strengthened my position within the family. I was becoming more than just a novice; I was proving myself as a capable and resourceful member of the organisation.

You become accustomed to that type of job, just as you become accustomed to witnessing blood, shit, and drugs on a daily basis. Additionally, the concept of hidden corpses, both in literature and as a proverb, comes to mind.

As I grew older, I began to question whether I would be able to continue working on that project indefinitely. Fortunately, I didn't have to worry about this question for too long, understanding that it was merely a learning experience to increase my familiarity with it and avoid committing to a single task for eternity.

Chapter 13

As I continued to grow and learn, I found myself questioning the path I was on more and more. The work at the port, while essential, was gruelling and often put me at odds with my own conscience. It was during one of these periods of introspection that Carlo approached me with a new opportunity—a chance to expand my responsibilities into a different part of our operations: nightclubs and bars.

"Silas," Carlo began one evening as we sat in his study, the room filled with the soft glow of lamplight. "I think it's time you took on a new challenge. You've proven yourself at the port, and now we need someone we can trust to manage our nightlife interests."

The idea intrigued me. The nightclubs and bars were a significant part of our income, providing not just money but also valuable connections and influence. They were places where deals were made, alliances were formed, and information was gathered. Managing these establishments would require a different set of skills—diplomacy, charisma, and a keen understanding of human nature.

"I'd be honoured, Don Carlo," I replied, feeling a mix of excitement and apprehension. "What do you need me to do?"

Carlo smiled, a rare expression of warmth from the usually stoic man. "Start by visiting each of our establishments. Get to know the managers, the staff, and the patrons. Understand the business from the ground up. And remember, these places are more than just sources of income—they're our eyes and ears in the city."

The next day, I began my new assignment. The first stop was La Rosa, one of our most popular nightclubs, known for its high-profile clientele and lavish atmosphere. As I walked through the doors, the thumping bass of the music and the vibrant energy of the crowd hit me like a wave. It was a stark contrast to the gritty, industrial feel of the port.

I was greeted by Marco, the manager, a suave and confident man who had been running the club for years. He gave me a tour of the place, pointing out the key areas—the VIP lounge, the main dance floor, the bar, and the back offices where more private transactions took place.

"Running a club like this is all about balance," Marco explained as we made our way through the crowded dance floor. "You need to keep the patrons happy, the staff motivated, and the business running smoothly. And, of course, you need to keep an eye out for any trouble."

I quickly realised that the nightclubs and bars were microcosms of our larger operations. They required the same vigilance, the same ability to read people and situations, and the same ruthlessness when necessary. But they also offered a different kind of satisfaction—a chance to see the immediate impact of our work in the smiles and laughter of the patrons, the pulse of the music, and the flow of money.

Over the next few weeks, I visited each of our establishments, getting to know the managers and staff and learning the intricacies of each place. There was The Blue Orchid, a more upscale bar catering to the city's elite; The Den, a gritty, underground club known for its live music and edgy vibe; and The Golden Lily, a more laid-back bar that was a favourite among locals.

Each place had its own unique atmosphere and clientele, but they all shared common challenges—keeping the business profitable, maintaining order, and ensuring that our interests were protected. I spent my days meeting with the managers, going over financial reports, and dealing with any issues that arose. My nights were spent observing the operations, mingling with patrons, and keeping a watchful eye on everything.

One of the biggest challenges was dealing with the various issues that arose—fights, thefts, and occasionally, more serious threats. It was a constant balancing act, maintaining a welcoming atmosphere while also projecting an air of authority and control.

One night at The Blue Orchid, a scuffle broke out between two patrons. I saw Marco trying to diffuse the situation, but it quickly escalated. I stepped in, my presence sufficient to calm things down. I escorted the troublemakers outside and made it clear that their behaviour wouldn't be tolerated.

"Thanks, Silas," Marco said afterward, a look of relief on his face. "Situations like that can get out of hand quickly."

"It's all part of the job," I replied, feeling a sense of satisfaction at having handled the situation smoothly.

As I settled into my new role, I began to see the nightclubs and bars not just as businesses but as vital parts of our network. They were places where information flowed freely; we could gather intelligence on rival families, corrupt officials, and potential threats. They were also places where we could build alliances, offering a safe and luxurious environment for our allies to meet and conduct their own business.

One evening, while overseeing operations at The Den, I met Cecilia again. She had become a regular at our clubs, her sharp wit and striking beauty making her a popular figure among the patrons. She greeted me with a warm smile, and we fell into easy conversation.

"Silas, it seems you're everywhere these days," she teased, her eyes twinkling with amusement.

"Just trying to keep things running smoothly," I replied coldly, while my face tensed, but she kept smiling as if she wouldn't notice it.

"Remember, Silas, these places are about more than just business. They're about people. Understand them, and you'll succeed." As if I didn't, I thought, almost rolling my eyes and nodding with a tight smile, hoping that she would disappear as soon as possible, limiting the chance that anyone would hear us."

I made it a point to get to know the staff and patrons in order to better understand their needs and concerns. I listened to their stories, their struggles, and their triumphs, and in doing so, I built a network of trust and loyalty that proved invaluable.

One of the most significant moments in my new role came when I was approached by a local politician, a regular at The Golden Lily. He had a problem—one that required discretion, and a solution that only someone in our position could provide. It was a delicate situation involving blackmail and political manoeuvring, and a careful and calculated response was required.

I met with Carlo to discuss the situation, outlining the potential risks and benefits. He listened carefully, his expression thoughtful.

"This is an opportunity, Silas," he said finally. "Handle it well, and we'll have a powerful ally. But be careful. One wrong move, and it could all blow up in our faces." He always said it calmly, not like we were talking about millions of dollars that could get lost in a deal-breaker.

I took his advice to heart, carefully planning each step of our response. I gathered information, met with key players, and orchestrated a solution that not only resolved the politician's problem but also strengthened our position.

That operation's success was a turning point for me. It demonstrated my ability to handle complex and high-stakes situations, earning me the respect and trust of Carlo and the other members of the family.

As time went on, I continued to juggle the various responsibilities of my role, from overseeing shipments at the port to managing our nightclubs and bars. Each day brought new challenges and new opportunities to prove myself. And through it all, I found a sense of purpose and belonging that I had never experienced before.

However, despite my success, I couldn't shake the nagging question of whether this was truly the life I wanted. The nightclubs and bars offered a glimpse of a different world—one filled with music, laughter, and human connection. It was a world that contrasted sharply with the mafia's shadows and secrecy. It was an unfamiliar world for me. While she was already working here, Cecilia easily went back and forth. At that time, I discovered that Cecilia was a few years older than she actually was, despite her seemingly youthful appearance, which is a rare trait in women. However, I learned to ignore her as best I could.

As I stood on the balcony of The Blue Orchid one evening, looking out over the bustling city, I felt a sense of longing and uncertainty. The path I had chosen was fraught with danger and moral ambiguity, but it was also filled with opportunities and possibilities.

I knew that my journey was far from over, and that the choices I made would shape not only my destiny but also the future of our family. And as I navigated the complexities of our world, I resolved to do so with integrity, determination, and a sense of purpose that would guide me through the challenges and triumphs ahead.

The transition to managing nightclubs and bars had opened my eyes to new possibilities and new ways of thinking. It had taught me valuable lessons about leadership, human nature, and the delicate balance of power. It had given me a renewed sense of hope and determination as I continued my journey through the intricate and dangerous world of the Mafia.

Another evening, after a particularly gruelling week of managing our nightclubs and bars, I found myself back at the family villa, longing for a moment of peace. As I stepped into the kitchen to grab a drink, I noticed my father, Sandey, sitting at the table, deep in thought. His presence was both comforting and unsettling; we hadn't had a heart-to-heart conversation in a while, and I sensed that tonight might be the night for one.

"Hey, Dad," I said, pulling out a chair and sitting down across from him.

"Silas," he replied, looking up with a hint of a smile. "How's everything going at the clubs?"

I sighed, running a hand through my hair. "It's... challenging. The challenges include managing people, keeping things running smoothly, and dealing with all the issues that come up. It's a lot."

Sandey nodded with a thoughtful expression. "I can imagine. It's a different kind of pressure, isn't it?"

"Yeah, it is," I admitted. "It's not just about the business. It's about the people, the environment, and the whole vibe of the place. It's intense."

He gave me a long, appraising look. "You've been handling it well, though. I've been hearing good things."

"Thanks," I said, feeling a surge of pride. "But sometimes, it feels like there's so much more to learn. And it's not always easy to figure out what's right, you know?"

"That's true," Sandey said, his tone serious. "This life, it's a lot to take on, especially at your age. But you're doing better than I could have hoped."

I hesitated for a moment before deciding to share something that had been weighing on my mind. My father had mentioned it repeatedly, and I knew his relationship to it—he didn't want to be here, nor did he like having me involved in all that. However, he felt compelled to involve me, as I was the only one who could provide me with protection. Too many years had passed here, and I knew too much about their business. "Dad, sometimes I wonder if this is really what I want. Being involved in all of this. It's... complicated."

Sandey sighed, leaning back in his chair. "I know, Silas. I know it's not easy. And I won't lie to you—there are dark parts of this life that can weigh heavily on your conscience. But there are also opportunities to make a difference, to steer things in a better direction."

I nodded, absorbing his words. "I've been thinking about that a lot. I'm trying to find my place and figure out how I can make a positive impact."

He smiled, a hint of sadness in his eyes. "You're already doing that, even if you don't see it. But I understand your struggle. It's important to find something that aligns with your values, something that gives you a sense of purpose."

There was a moment of silence, and the weight of our conversation settled between us. Then Sandey leaned forward, his expression more serious than before.

"Silas, there's something I need to talk to you about," he began. "You remember Dr. Russo, right? Did you recently lose your family doctor?

I nodded. Dr. Russo had been with the family for as long as I could remember, a trusted and familiar figure. His sudden death had been a shock to all of us, which is why nobody ever talked about it. "Yeah, I remember. It was a big loss."

Sandey's expression darkened. "I have reason to believe that his death wasn't natural. There were some unusual circumstances surrounding it."

A chill ran down my spine. "What do you mean?"

"There are rumours," he said quietly. "Rumours suggest that he was silenced because he knew too much or because he crossed the wrong people." "Either way, it left us without a doctor, and we need someone we can trust."

I stared at him, processing the implications of what he was saying. "You think I should be the new doctor?"

Sandey shook his head. "No, not exactly. But I think you could play a crucial role in finding and managing a new one. You should be someone who aligns with our values and can handle the complexities of our world."

The idea intrigued me. It was a chance to make a real difference, to ensure that the health and well-being of our people were looked after by someone trustworthy and competent. It was a role that felt more in line with my values, a way to use my skills for something positive.

"I like the sound of that," I said slowly. "It feels... purposeful. It feels like something I can really get behind."

Sandey smiled with a look of pride in his eyes. "I'm glad to hear that, Silas. I know it's a big responsibility, but I think you're ready for it. And who knows, maybe this will lead to even greater things down the line."

I nodded, feeling a renewed sense of determination. "I'll do it, Dad. I'll find the right person and make sure they understand what it means to be part of our family."

As we continued to talk, I felt a weight lift off my shoulders. This new role offered a sense of purpose and alignment with my values that I hadn't felt in any of my other responsibilities. It was a way to honour Dr. Russo's memory and ensure that our family was cared for by someone who truly understood the importance of their role.

The conversation with my father had given me a new direction and a new sense of meaning in the chaotic world I was navigating. And as I looked ahead to the future, I felt a sense of hope and determination. This was a role I could embrace wholeheartedly, one that aligned with my values and allowed me to make a real difference. The only challenge would be to make Carlo appreciate this idea, too.

That night, as I lay in bed, I couldn't help but think about the journey ahead. There would be challenges, no doubt, but there would also be opportunities to learn, grow, and make a positive impact. And for the first time in a long while, I felt a sense of clarity about my path.

With my father's support and the lessons I had learned so far, I was ready to take on this new challenge and make it my own. The future was uncertain, but I knew that with determination and purpose, I could navigate whatever lay ahead. And in that moment, I felt a deep sense of gratitude for the opportunity to make a difference in the lives of those around me.

Chapter 14

Every single day had reminded me that I did not want to be here. Still, I would go, avoiding the conversation I had to have to come away from here. It was good enough that I did that, since it might have been rare for me to ask Carlo for anything like that anyway. Instead, my father ordered everything, which unfortunately meant that I would have to discuss it with him on my own. I didn't want to feel like I had let Carlo down, especially when I could see that my father was more than happy with my choice. I wondered why they always chose my birthday for such a special occasion, but I didn't ask. The day that others celebrated for themselves had already turned into a day I desperately wanted to skip, as if it had never happened.

It was another busy day in the family business, and I had come home a bit earlier than usual. My father was away on a working trip, and the house was quieter than usual. Carlo had asked me to meet him in his office, a request that filled me with a mix of anticipation and dread.

As I walked into his office, Carlo was already sitting behind his desk, his eyes fixed on some documents in front of him. He looked up as I entered, his expression unreadable.

"Silas, sit down," he said, his voice calm yet authoritative.

I sat down, my heart pounding. I had a feeling I knew what this was about, but I wasn't ready to bring it up myself.

Carlo leaned back in his chair; his gaze intense. "Your father tells me you have something you want to discuss."

I swallowed hard, trying to steady my nerves. "Yes, Carlo. I've been thinking a lot about my future."

He raised an eyebrow, waiting for me to continue.

"I... I want to pursue an education in medicine," I said, the words feeling heavy in the air between us. "I want to become a doctor."

Carlo's expression darkened, and he leaned forward, resting his elbows on the desk. "A doctor? Silas, you are aware of the responsibilities you have here. The family relies on you."

"I know, Carlo," I said quickly. "I'm not trying to abandon my responsibilities. I want to find a way to balance both. I want to help people in a different way, to make a positive impact."

Carlo sighed, rubbing his temples. "Do you understand what you're asking for? Medical school is demanding, and it requires full commitment. How do you plan to balance that with your duties here?"

"I believe I can do it," I replied, trying to sound confident. "I can manage my time and ensure that I fulfil my responsibilities to the family while pursuing my education."

Carlo's eyes bore into mine, filled with a mixture of disappointment and frustration. "Silas, this is not just about you. The family needs you here, fully committed. What if your studies conflict with your work? What if you become distracted?"

"I won't let that happen," I promised. "I will make sure to prioritise my duties here. On the other side, I also need to follow my passion and do something meaningful with my life."

Carlo was silent for a long moment, his gaze unwavering. "Does your father endorse this?"

I nodded. "Yes, of course he does." Carlo leaned back in his chair, contemplating. "Silas, I care about you. You're like a son to me. I want what's best for you, but I also need to ensure the stability of the family."

"I understand," I said, my voice steady while my mind ran wild. He never pointed out that I was like a son to him. "And I promise, I won't let you down. I will find a way to balance both."

Carlo sighed again, a long, weary exhale. "Very well but understand this: if I see that you are neglecting your duties here, this arrangement will end. You have to prove to me that you can handle both responsibilities."

"Thank you, Carlo," I said, relief washing over me. "I won't let you down."

"I hope not," Carlo replied, his voice stern. "Because if you do, there will be consequences. Now go, and make sure you balance this carefully."

I stood up, feeling a mixture of relief and determination. As I left Carlo's office, I knew that the road ahead would be challenging, but I was ready to face it. This was my chance to follow my passion while still honouring my commitments to the family. And I was determined to succeed, no matter what it took.

As I stepped outside, the cool evening air greeted me, a stark contrast to the tense atmosphere inside. I couldn't help but feel a sense of liberation, a newfound sense of purpose. My path was clear now, and I was ready to take on the challenge.

The conversation with Carlo had been tough but necessary. It had forced me to confront my fears and doubts, as well as articulate my desires and ambitions. And doing so gave me the strength to pursue my dreams.

In the days that followed, I threw myself into my studies with renewed vigour, determined to prove myself. I balanced my responsibilities in the family business with my coursework, finding a rhythm that allowed me to excel in both areas.

And as the months passed, I found myself growing more confident and capable. The challenges were immense, but they only fuelled my determination. I knew that I was on the right path, and I was committed to seeing it through.

I understood that I would stay here indefinitely as a reliable family member. All the stories I had heard about the other world described a strange place that I would never have the opportunity to visit. I was too loyal, goal-oriented, and strict with myself to even consider being there any day.

Every single day reminded me that I didn't want to be here. Yet I continued, avoiding the conversation I dreaded. Asking Carlo for anything was rare, and my father, Sandey, always ordered everything instead. Unfortunately, that didn't exclude the fact that I had to talk to him about it myself. I hated feeling like I had disappointed Carlo, even as I saw the satisfaction on my father's face. I wondered why they always chose my birthday for such matters, but never asked. I desperately wanted to skip over what others celebrated, as if it had never existed.

Every day at my private medical school was a grind. I worked closely with my tutor, Dr. Ferrara, a stern yet brilliant mentor. The study was intense; there were no other students, just a relentless focus on me. The hours were long, and the material was challenging, but I persevered.

Dr. Ferrara had a habit of testing me with rapid-fire questions. "What is the primary function of the hippocampus, Silas?"

"Memory consolidation," I answered, my mind always on high alert.

"Correct. And what is the difference between an artery and a vein?"

"Arteries carry oxygenated blood away from the heart, while veins carry deoxygenated blood towards the heart," I responded, my voice steady.

The days blurred together, each one a testament to my commitment. Every morning, I trained for two hours before heading to my study. The physical training kept me grounded, a necessary counterbalance to the mental strain.

Sometimes, the weight of it all felt unbearable. The dual demands of the family business and my studies put me under pressure. But I knew I had to push through. I couldn't afford to fail.

One evening, as I was wrapping up my work at one of the family's nightclubs, my father, Sandey, approached me. He had that familiar look of concern mixed with pride.

"Silas, do you have some time?" he asked, his voice gentle.

"Of course, Dad," I replied, following him to a quieter corner of the club.

We sat down, and he looked at me with a mixture of curiosity and worry. "How are you feeling about everything? Balancing the family business and your studies?"

I sighed, running a hand through my hair. "It's tough, Dad. Sometimes I feel like I'm being pulled in two different directions. But I know this is what I want. Becoming a doctor feels like my true calling."

Sandey nodded thoughtfully. "I understand. It's not easy to juggle both. But I want you to know that I'm proud of you for following your passion."

"Thanks, Dad," I said, feeling a swell of gratitude. "It means a lot to me."

That might have been the only, or at least the longest, conversation I had that year with either of them. Everything else revolved around work and study, and I continued to train for two hours each morning, as I had done in previous years.

Sometimes, training was the only thing to look forward to, while everything else made my head, heart, or entire body ache. I understood that I would stay here indefinitely as a reliable family member. Everything I had been told about the other world was a strange place I would never get to see. I was too loyal, goal-oriented, and strict with myself to even consider being there any day.

A normal day in my life started before dawn. The alarm clock buzzed sharply at 5:00 AM, a sound I had grown accustomed to over the years. Training always came first. It was my grounding ritual, a way to centre myself before the chaos of the day began.

Jarle, my combat instructor, was already waiting for me in the gym. He was a towering figure with a stern expression, a former Special Forces operative who had been with our family for years. Our training sessions were gruelling, a mix of karate, aikido, tai chi, and other martial arts. Jarle didn't go easy on me, and I didn't want him to.

"Ready, Silas?" Jarle inquired as he tossed me a pair of gloves.

"Always," I replied, tightening the straps.

For the next two hours, we went through a rigorous routine. Punches, kicks, throws, and holds—each movement had to be precise and powerful. Jarle's commands were sharp, and his corrections were immediate. It was in these moments of physical exertion that I found a rare clarity. The outside world faded, and there was only the next move, the next breath.

By 7:30 a.m., training was over. My muscles ached, but it was a familiar pain, one that reminded me of my progress. After a quick shower and a protein shake, I dressed and headed to my study session with Dr. Ferrara.

Dr. Ferrara's study was located in a quiet part of town, far from the bustling streets and prying eyes. It was a private arrangement, just the two of us. He was a man of few words, but his knowledge was vast, and he demanded excellence.

"Good morning, Silas," he greeted me as I walked in.

"Good morning, Dr. Ferrara," I replied, setting my bag down and pulling out my notes.

Our sessions were intense. Dr. Ferrara had a way of drilling information into me, asking rapid-fire questions that kept me on my toes.

"Explain the process of glycolysis," he asked.

"Glycolysis is the metabolic pathway that converts glucose into pyruvate, releasing energy and forming ATP," I answered, my mind racing to recall every detail.

"And what is the role of NAD+ in this process?"

"NAD+ acts as an electron carrier, becoming NADH in the process, which is then used in the electron transport chain to produce ATP," I continued.

Dr. Ferrara nodded, satisfied with my answers, but there was no time to relax. He moved on to the next topic, and then the next, pushing me to absorb as much as possible.

By noon, my brain felt as exhausted as my body had that morning. However, there was no time to rest. The family business required my attention, and I had to switch gears quickly. I grabbed a quick lunch on the way to our main office, a sleek, modern building that stood in stark contrast to the traditional, clandestine nature of our operations.

As I walked into the office, the atmosphere was buzzing with activity. Our staff was busy handling various tasks, from financial management to logistics and security. I headed straight to my desk, where a stack of reports and files awaited me. Today, I was tasked with reviewing our recent investments and planning for upcoming ventures.

"Silas, we need to go over the new deal with the overseas partners," Maria, our head of international operations, informed me as she approached my desk. She was efficient and sharp, someone I respected immensely.

"Let's go to the conference room," I replied, grabbing my notes and following her.

In the conference room, we were joined by several other key members of our team. We discussed the details of the deal, weighing the risks and benefits. My role was to analyse the financial aspects and ensure that everything aligned with our strategic goals.

"These projections look solid," I said, pointing to a chart on the screen. "But we need to consider the political climate in that region. It could affect our operations."

"Agreed," Maria nodded. "We'll have our local contacts keep us updated. But we need your final approval on this, sir."

I took a deep breath, considering the implications. "Let's proceed but keep a close watch on any developments. We need to be ready to adapt if necessary."

The meeting continued for another hour, covering various aspects of our international operations. By the time it ended, my head was spinning with information, but I felt a sense of accomplishment. Balancing my responsibilities was challenging, but I was proving to myself and to Carlo that I could handle it.

By late afternoon, I wrapped up my work at the office and headed to one of our nightclubs. This was part of my nightly routine, ensuring that our establishments were running smoothly and addressing any issues that arose.

The nightclub was already filling up with patrons by the time I arrived. The music was loud, the lights were flashing, and the atmosphere was electric. I made my way through the crowd, greeting familiar faces and keeping an eye out for anything unusual.

At the bar, I found Vinnie, the club manager. "How's everything tonight?" I asked, leaning in to hear him over the music.

"All good so far, Silas," Vinnie replied. "No troublemakers, and the night's just getting started."

"Good. Keep me posted if anything comes up," I said, patting him on the shoulder.

I made my rounds, checking in with the staff and ensuring that our security measures were in place. It was a delicate balance, maintaining a welcoming atmosphere while also keeping things under control. This was part of the family business that required a keen eye and a steady hand. However, despite the immense pressure I was under, I understood the importance of this task. Once I began working here as a doctor, I might not have much time, but I wouldn't have to put in endless hours. I was starting to look forward to that, since my hand warmed already, fire searching the midst of me.

Chapter 15

As the days turned into weeks and then months, my routine remained largely unchanged. Each morning began with a gruelling training session with Jarle, followed by a marathon study session with Dr. Ferrara. Then, it was off to the family business, where I spent the rest of the day overseeing operations at our various establishments.

My interaction with Cecilia was one aspect of my daily routine that I had grown accustomed to—and, truth be told, was not particularly fond of. She was a regular fixture at the nightclub, having worked there before I even joined the family business. While she was undeniably attractive and had always harboured a crush on me, I had never reciprocated her feelings.

Cecilia had a way of flirting with me that bordered on relentless, but I made it a point to keep our interactions strictly professional. I didn't want to encourage her advances, knowing that it would only complicate matters further. Despite my efforts to keep her at arm's length, Cecilia seemed determined to break through my defences.

One evening, as I was making my rounds at the club, I spotted Cecilia leaning against the bar, a coy smile playing on her lips. I tried to avoid making eye contact, but she caught my gaze and waved me over.

"Silas, darling, come join me for a drink," she purred, gesturing to the empty seat beside her.

I hesitated for a moment, considering my options. I could politely decline and continue with my rounds, or I could indulge her and risk sending the wrong message. In the end, I decided to err on the side of caution and approached her reluctantly.

"Hey, Cecilia." I greeted her with a forced smile, taking a seat beside her.

"Long time, no see," she said, flashing me a playful grin. "You've been avoiding me, haven't you?"

I shifted uncomfortably in my seat, unsure of how to respond. "I've just been busy with work; you know how it is."

Cecilia leaned in closer, her perfume wafting over me. "I've missed our little chats. You used to be so much more fun."

I forced a chuckle, trying to keep the mood light. "Well, you know how it is. Work comes first."

Cecilia's smile faltered slightly, and I could sense a hint of disappointment in her eyes. But before she could respond, I excused myself, citing some urgent business that required my attention.

As I made my way through the club, I couldn't shake the feeling of guilt that lingered in the pit of my stomach. I hated having to brush Cecilia off like that, but I knew it was for the best. Our relationship, if you could even call it that, was strictly professional, and I had no intention of letting it escalate into something more.

Weeks turned into months, and before I knew it, half a year had passed. During that time, I had become even more deeply entrenched in the family business, taking on additional responsibilities and duties. It seemed that Carlo had taken notice of my dedication and hard work, as he called me into his office one afternoon to discuss my future within the organisation.

"Silas, have a seat," Carlo said, gesturing to the chair across from his desk.

I took a seat, my heart pounding with anticipation. I had a feeling I knew what this meeting was about, but I didn't want to get ahead of myself.

"Silas, over the past few months, you've proven yourself to be a valuable asset to the family," Carlo began, his voice grave.

I nodded, silently urging him to continue.

"As you know, with great power comes great responsibility," Carlo said, his eyes locking with mine. "And I believe you're ready for the next step."

I swallowed hard, feeling a surge of excitement and apprehension coursing through me. "What do you mean?"

Carlo leaned forward, clasping his hands together on the desk. "I'm promoting you to the position of operations strategist."

My heart skipped a beat at the news. This was the opportunity I had been waiting for—a chance to prove myself on an even larger scale within the organization. But with that came a new set of challenges and responsibilities that I would have to navigate.

"Thank you, Carlo," I said, my voice tinged with gratitude. "I won't let you down."

Carlo nodded with a hint of pride in his eyes. "I know you won't. You've already proven yourself to be a valuable asset to the family, Silas. I have no doubt that you'll excel in this new role."

As I left Carlo's office, a sense of determination washed over me. This was my chance to make a real impact and carve out a legacy within the family business. I was determined to seize it with both hands.

In the days that followed, I immersed myself in my new role as operations strategist. My responsibilities expanded beyond the confines of the nightclub, encompassing all aspects of the family's operations. From overseeing our legitimate businesses to coordinating our illicit activities, I was involved in every facet of our enterprise.

One of the perks of my new position was the freedom it afforded me. No longer tied to a specific location or establishment, I was free to work from wherever I pleased. This newfound flexibility allowed me to spend more time focusing on my studies while still fulfilling my duties to the family.

However, with this newfound freedom came a sense of isolation. Gone were the days of camaraderie and companionship at the club, replaced instead by solitary hours spent poring over spreadsheets and reports. I missed the hustle and bustle of the nightclub, as well as the adrenaline rush of overseeing operations firsthand.

However, as much as I missed the excitement of the club, I knew that my new role was where I belonged. I was no longer just a cog in the machine; I was an integral part of the family business, entrusted with important responsibilities and duties. And I was determined to prove myself worthy of Carlo's trust and confidence.

Cecilia and I crossed paths less frequently now that I was no longer tied to the nightclub. And while I couldn't deny that I felt a pang of guilt at the thought of brushing her off, I knew that it was for the best. Our relationship had always been complex, and she remained one of the few individuals with whom I could speak more freely due to her extensive knowledge from her own family's organization. Still, I didn't want to risk jeopardising my newfound position within the mafia.

As the months passed, I settled into my new role as operations strategist. Each day brought with it new challenges and opportunities, but I faced them head-on with determination and resolve. I was no longer just a foot soldier in the family business; I was a leader, responsible for shaping the direction of our organisation.

As I looked to the future, I knew that there would be many more challenges ahead. But I was ready to face them head-on, armed with the knowledge and experience I had gained along the way. With Carlo's guidance and support, I was confident that I could overcome any obstacle that stood in my way.

The first year came almost to an end as I found myself in Carlo's office again. It had been a long time since I had been here before, but it was one of the few times I had seen him at all. Unlike the last time, I was eager to see him again.

Carlo was seated behind his desk, poring over a stack of reports, when I entered. He looked up as I approached, his expression unreadable. I took a seat opposite him, my nerves tingling with anticipation.

"Silas," Carlo greeted me, his voice a rumble that filled the room. "It's good to see you. How's the new role treating you?"

I straightened up in my chair, gathering my thoughts. "It's been a learning experience, to say the least. But I think we've made some significant strides this year."

Carlo nodded, his gaze penetrating. "I've been keeping an eye on your progress. You've handled yourself well, Silas. You've proven yourself capable."

I felt a swell of pride in his words, but I knew better than to let it show too much. "Thank you, Carlo. I've done my best to live up to your expectations."

Carlo leaned back in his chair, steeping his fingers in front of him. "Indeed, you have. This brings us to the reason you're present here today."

I braced myself, sensing that this conversation would be pivotal. "Yes, Carlo?"

Carlo fixed me with a steady gaze. "I've been thinking about your future within the organisation, Silas. You've shown tremendous growth and potential, and I believe it's time to expand your responsibilities even further."

I blinked in surprise, not quite sure what he was getting at. "Expand my responsibilities?"

Carlo nodded. "Indeed. I want you to start taking a more active role in our international operations. We have interests overseas that could benefit from your strategic oversight."

I swallowed hard, my mind racing. International operations would mean dealing with a whole new set of challenges and risks, but it would also be an opportunity to prove myself on a global scale. On the other side, my time would go from limited to no free time at all.

"I understand," I replied carefully. "I'm honoured by your trust, Carlo. I won't let you down."

Carlo's expression softened, a rare hint of a smile playing at his lips. "I know you won't, Silas, but this won't be without its challenges. You'll need to be prepared to travel and adapt to new environments and cultures."

"I'm ready," I assured him, my determination clear. "I've been preparing for this."

Carlo nodded approvingly. "Good. I'll have my assistant send you details of your first assignment. I expect you to leave within the week."

I nodded, my mind already teeming with plans and preparations, as I contemplated the transition to digital studies. Not that I wasn't good at it, but I wondered if my mentor would be able to adjust to this new role. "Understood, Carlo. I'll make sure everything is in order."

Carlo dismissed me with a nod, and as I left his office, I couldn't help but feel a mix of excitement and trepidation. This was the opportunity I had been waiting for—a chance to prove myself on an international stage. But it also meant leaving behind the familiar comforts of home and facing unknown dangers in far-off lands. I loved it. Since I flew home last time, I had been looking forward to traveling again and again.

In the days that followed, I threw myself into preparations for my first international assignment. I spent hours poring over maps and intelligence reports, familiarising myself with the political landscape and cultural nuances of the region I would be operating in.

As I packed my bags for the journey ahead, I couldn't shake the feeling of nervous anticipation. This was a new chapter in my life, one that would test my skills and resilience like never before. On the other hand, I was determined to succeed, to make Carlo proud and prove that I was worthy of the trust he had placed in me, while he challenged me to have both my studies and the work effort, he wanted from me at once.

Before I knew it, the day of departure arrived. I stood on the tarmac of a private airstrip, watching as the sleek jet prepared for take-off. Beside me, Carlo stood silently, his presence a comforting reassurance amid the whirlwind of emotions I was feeling.

"Safe travels, Silas," Carlo said, clapping me on the shoulder. "Remember everything you've learned. Trust your instincts."

"I will," I replied, my voice steady despite the rare feeling in my stomach. "Thank you, Carlo, for this opportunity."

Carlo nodded; his gaze unwavering. "You've earned it, Silas. Now go and show them what you're made of."

With that, I boarded the plane, ready to face whatever challenges lay ahead. As the jet soared into the sky, I couldn't help but feel a surge of excitement and determination. This was my chance to make a name for myself and prove that I was more than just a foot soldier in the family business.

Chapter 16

Months passed as I immersed myself in my new role, navigating the complexities of international operations with a mixture of caution and determination. I travelled from country to country, meeting with local contacts, negotiating deals, and overseeing operations on behalf of the family.

One evening, as I was reviewing some documents in my hotel room, there was a knock on the door. I opened it to find Cecilia standing there, a tentative smile on her face.

"Silas," she greeted me softly. "Can we talk?"

I hesitated for a moment, unsure of what to say. But curiosity got the better of me, and I stepped aside to let her in.

Cecilia entered, closing the door behind her. She looked around the room, her gaze lingering on the stacks of papers and files scattered across the desk.

"It's been a while," she said, her voice tinged with nostalgia. "Since we last spoke."

I nodded, and my throat suddenly dried. "Yeah, it has."

Cecilia took a deep breath, as if gathering her thoughts. "I wanted to apologise, Silas. For how I acted before. I know I came on strong, and I didn't mean to make you uncomfortable."

I glanced at her, surprised by her candidness. "It's... it's okay, Cecilia. You were just doing your job."

She shook her head, her expression earnest. "No, Silas. It was more than that. I liked you, and I thought... well, never mind."

There was a moment of silence between us, the air thick with unspoken words. I could see the vulnerability in her eyes, and it softened something inside of me.

"Cecilia," I began, my voice gentle. "You didn't do anything wrong. I appreciate your honesty."

She then looked at me, her gaze searching. "Do you?"

I nodded. "Yes, I do, but things have changed now, Cecilia. I'm not... I'm not the same person I was back then."

Cecilia nodded slowly, as if coming to terms with my words. "I understand."

For a moment, we stood there in silence, the weight of our past hanging between us. And then, unexpectedly, Cecilia smiled.

"Well, I just wanted to clear the air," she said, her voice light. "I won't keep you any longer. Good luck with everything, Silas."

I returned her smile, feeling a sense of closure settle over me. "Thank you, Cecilia. Take care."

With that, she turned and left, closing the door softly behind her. As I watched her go, I couldn't help but feel a sense of gratitude for her understanding.

As my international assignments continued, I found myself growing more confident and capable in my role as operations strategist. I travelled to various countries, from bustling cities to remote outposts, overseeing operations and forging alliances on behalf of the family.

Carlo kept a close eye on my progress, offering guidance and support when needed. He was pleased with my performance, but he never let me forget the weight of my responsibilities. Each success was followed by new challenges, and each opportunity was tempered by risks that loomed on the horizon.

Through it all, I remained focused and determined. I juggled my duties with precision, balancing the demands of the family business and my studies in medicine. It was a challenging and sometimes isolating existence, but it was one that I had chosen for myself.

One day, I came to another meeting in a different country, far away from home. The past few days had been exhausting, and I had learned as much as never before, even in school. However, at that time, it was different.

Some of my colleagues, or more accurately, other family members, had already informed me that I should eagerly anticipate this meeting, as the leader always brings something special with him. I didn't waste a single thought on that before I entered the castle, which he had invited me into.

Initially, I didn't notice anything unusual; I simply pursued them across the expansive palace. As we approached a large, closed door, he would take a few moments to locate the correct key and unlock it.

Inside, I struggled at first to remain my calm, unaffected self, illuminated by what I saw. To have several women at such a meeting wasn't anything unusual; in some places they were even my age or younger, which showed the power they had and how unaffected they were from any kind of law.

However, this was not the case here. There were between twenty and thirty women, all of whom were gorgeous, especially in the way they dressed. It wasn't that they were all naked, like usual; no, they would sometimes even be almost fully dressed beside those essential parts, which are normally hidden and shown.

I remained as calm as I could and went to the place that was meant for me. The women wouldn't start with anything they had not asked for. Ten women stood in a row, silently rising to their feet. Some others bound each other in intricate knots, prompting me to question whether this was a directive or a personal preference.

At least you saw that they were not unhappy about it. Even from my position, I could see that their spot was more than ready to be used.

The leader of this meeting, Don Marcelo, stood at the head of the room, his presence commanding and authoritative. He was a man of imposing stature, with a sharp mind and an even sharper gaze. As I settled into my seat, I couldn't help but feel a mix of fascination and curiosity about what was to come.

Don Marcelo began the meeting with a brief introduction, welcoming everyone and outlining the agenda for the day. The room was filled with powerful men from various parts of the world, all of them here to discuss business, alliances, and strategies.

"Welcome, gentlemen," Don Marcelo began, his voice resonating through the room. "Today, we have much to discuss. Our operations are expanding, and with expansion come new challenges and opportunities."

He paused, allowing his words to sink in before continuing. "First on the agenda is the distribution of our new product line. We have developed a high-quality batch that is ready to hit the market. Our partners in South America have ensured that the purity is unmatched, and we need to strategize on the best routes and methods for distribution."

One of the men, Don Miguel, a well-respected figure in the organisation, spoke up. "Don Marcelo, we have secured routes through Central America that should facilitate smooth transport. However, we need to ensure that our contacts in customs are well compensated to avoid any issues."

"Indeed," Don Marcelo agreed. "Bribery and maintaining loyalty are keys. We must ensure that our financial resources are allocated effectively. Silas," he said, turning his attention to me. "What are your thoughts on this?"

I cleared my throat, feeling the weight of the room's attention on me. "I believe that diversifying our routes can mitigate risks. Relying too heavily on a single path can make us vulnerable. We should consider alternate routes through the Caribbean, where we have less oversight and more control."

Don Marcelo nodded appreciatively. "Wise words, Silas. Diversification is crucial. We shall allocate resources to explore and secure these additional routes."

As the discussion continued, topics ranged from supply chain management to security measures. Each speaker brought valuable insights, and the collaborative nature of the meeting was evident. The organisation operated like a well-oiled machine, with each part contributing to the whole.

After a while, the conversation shifted to a more sensitive topic: the handling of competitors and rivals. This was a subject that always carried an air of tension and seriousness.

"Recent intelligence has indicated that our rivals on the East Coast are planning to expand their operations into our territory," Don Marcelo stated. "We cannot allow this encroachment. We need a strategy to neutralise this threat."

Don Franco, another influential member, leaned forward. "We have operatives in place who can gather more detailed intelligence on their movements. Once we have a clearer picture, we can plan a pre-emptive strike to disrupt their operations."

"Good," Don Marcelo replied. "We need to be proactive. Silas, you've been learning the ropes very quickly. What would you suggest as a pre-emptive measure?"

I took a deep breath, considering my response carefully. "We could use misinformation to our advantage. Plant false intelligence about a large shipment or a vulnerable position in our network. If they take the bait, we can ambush them, dealing a significant blow to their operations."

Don Marcelo's eyes gleamed with approval. "An excellent strategy, Silas. Deception and surprise are powerful tools. We shall implement this plan and see how our rivals respond."

The meeting continued, covering various aspects of the organisation's operations, from financial management to recruitment strategies. Despite the gravity of the discussions, there was an underlying camaraderie among the men. They were bound by a common goal and a shared sense of purpose.

As the meeting drew to a close, Don Marcelo addressed the room once more. "Gentlemen, we have made significant progress today. Our organisation is strong because of each and every one of you. Remember, our strength lies in our unity and adaptability. Let us continue to work together to secure our future."

With that, the meeting concluded, and the men began to disperse, engaging in smaller conversations and networking. I took the opportunity to approach Don Marcelo, feeling a mix of respect and curiosity.

"Don Marcelo, thank you for including me in this meeting," I said. "It was incredibly insightful."

He smiled, placing a hand on my shoulder. "You did well, Silas. Your contributions were valuable. I see great potential in you. Continue to learn and grow, and you will go far in this organisation."

"Thank you, sir," I replied, feeling a sense of pride and determination.

As I made my way out of the castle, my mind was buzzing with the day's events. The world of organised crime was complex and multifaceted, and I was beginning to understand the intricacies involved. There was a certain allure to it—a sense of power and control that was both intoxicating and daunting.

However, amidst the discussions of strategy and power, there was also a glimpse into another aspect of this world: the presence of women and the underlying dynamics of control and submission. It was a stark reminder of the darker side of this life, one that I was still trying to fully comprehend.

As I walked through the dimly lit corridors, I couldn't help but think about the women I had seen earlier. Their presence at the meeting, as well as the way they dressed and tied up, left a lasting impression on me. There was a part of me that was curious, wanting to understand more about that aspect of the world.

The journey back to my accommodations was quiet, giving me time to reflect. The life I had chosen was filled with contradictions: power and vulnerability, control and submission, respect and fear. It was a delicate balance, one that required constant vigilance and adaptability.

The days that followed were filled with more meetings and discussions. Each day brought new challenges and opportunities, and I continued to learn and grow under the guidance of the experienced men around me. I was determined to navigate the world of organised crime with the same resolve and dedication that had brought me this far, despite its challenging nature.

As time passed, I found myself becoming more comfortable in my role. The initial apprehension gave way to a sense of purpose and confidence. The organisation valued my insights and contributions, and I began to feel like an integral part of the team.

One evening, after a particularly intense meeting, I found myself alone with Don Marcelo. He had taken a liking to me, often offering guidance and mentorship.

"Silas," he said, his tone thoughtful. "You have a keen mind and a sharp instinct. Have you ever considered specialising in a particular area within our organisation?"

I hesitated, unsure of how to respond. "I'm not sure, Don Marcelo. There are many aspects of this life that intrigue me, but I haven't decided on a specific path yet."

He nodded, his eyes piercing. "That's understandable. Take your time to explore and learn. But remember, specialisation can give you an edge and make you indispensable. Think about what truly interests you and where you can make the most impact."

His words stayed with me, prompting me to reflect on my journey so far. There were many facets to the organisation, each with its own challenges and rewards. The key was to find where my skills and interests aligned and carve out a niche for myself.

As I lay in bed that night, my mind wandered back to the women I had seen at the meeting. There was something about that dynamic—the power, the control, and the intricate dance of dominance and submission—that intrigued me. It was a world within a world, one that required a different set of skills and understanding.

Chapter 17

We are almost here in the present time now. While this last chapter will talk about everything I've been through throughout the year, since may have been particularly challenging because I was no longer a young boy in need of education or work experience. No. Now, I found myself in a precarious situation where I had to make a decision between my father and Don Carlo, each with a distinct vision for the future. Our final meeting is scheduled for tomorrow. As a result, I will write you as quickly as possible about the complex challenges that have crossed my mind.

The year began with a sense of newfound responsibility. I was no longer just an observer or a learner; I was an active participant in the world of organised crime. The transition was jarring. I found myself juggling the demands of my father, who saw me continuing in the family business, and Don Carlo, who had groomed me for a different role within the organization. The clash of their visions was palpable, and I was caught in the middle, trying to navigate my way through a maze of expectations and responsibilities.

My days started early and ended late. I was up before dawn, reviewing shipments and ensuring the smooth operation of our logistics network. The port had become my domain, and I took pride in running it efficiently. Every day brought new challenges: customs officials demanding higher bribes, rival gangs trying to muscle in on our territory, and the constant threat of law enforcement. I had to stay sharp, making quick decisions and adapting to ever-changing circumstances.

Balancing my duties at the port with my studies was no small feat. I had decided to pursue a degree in operations management, believing that a formal education would provide me with the tools to run our operations more effectively. The coursework was rigorous, often requiring me to study logistics theories and supply chain management principles late into the night. My professors knew me as a diligent student, but they had no idea of the double life I was leading.

The pressure was relentless. I was expected to excel academically while maintaining my responsibilities within the organization. My father was pleased with my dedication to the family business, but he was unaware of my academic pursuits. I feared his reaction if he discovered that I was dividing my time and energy between two worlds. Don Carlo, on the other hand, was supportive of my education. He viewed it as an asset—something that would make me more valuable to the organization in the long run.

Weekends were non-existent for me. While my peers enjoyed their free time, I was either buried in textbooks or dealing with crises at the port. My social life was practically non-existent. The few friends I did have drifted away, unable to understand the demands on my time. Loneliness became a constant companion, but I had no choice but to press on. I was driven by a sense of duty and a desire to prove myself.

The stakes were high, and failure was not an option. Every decision I made had consequences, not just for me but for the entire organization. There were moments when I doubted myself, questioning whether I was cut out for this life. The weight of responsibility was overwhelming, and I often felt like I was walking a tightrope, one misstep away from disaster.

Despite the challenges, there were moments of triumph. Successfully negotiating a deal with a rival gang, outsmarting customs officials, and ensuring the timely delivery of shipments brought a sense of accomplishment. Each victory was a reminder of why I had chosen this path. I was good at what I did, and my contributions were making a difference.

Don Carlo continued to mentor me, providing guidance and support. He recognised the toll that the dual responsibilities were taking on me and often advised me to find a balance. "Silas," he would say, "you have a sharp mind and a strong will. Use them to your advantage. Don't let the pressure break you. Learn to manage your time and prioritise."

His words were a source of comfort, but finding that balance was easier said than done. There were days when I felt like I was on the verge of collapse; my mind and body were pushed to their limits. Sleep was a luxury I could rarely afford, and the constant stress took a toll on my health. I was perpetually exhausted, running on sheer determination and caffeine.

As the months passed, the tension between my father and Don Carlo's visions for my future grew more pronounced. My father wanted me to take on a more prominent role within the family business, focusing solely on expanding our operations and solidifying our power. Don Carlo, however, saw the value in my education and believed that I could bring a new level of sophistication to our operations with my knowledge and skills.

The conflicting expectations weighed heavily on me. I respected both men immensely and didn't want to disappoint either of them. My father's traditional approach was rooted in loyalty and family ties, while Don Carlo's forward-thinking mindset emphasised innovation and strategic planning. I was torn between the two, struggling to find a path that would honour both their wishes and my own aspirations.

In the midst of this internal conflict, I discovered a new facet of our operations: the world of BDSM. It was an aspect that had always been present, but one that I had not fully understood. I was fascinated by the women at the meetings, the power dynamics, and the control. It was a world within a world, with its own rules and complexities. I began to see how the principles of dominance and submission paralleled the power struggles within our organisation.

This realisation opened my eyes to the broader implications of control and influence. I started to apply these principles to my role as an operations strategist. Understanding the motivations and desires of those around me became crucial. I learned to navigate the intricate web of relationships and power dynamics, using them to my advantage.

The more I delved into this aspect, the more I realised its potential. It wasn't just about physical control; it was about psychological manipulation and strategic positioning. I began to see how I could use this knowledge to strengthen our operations and outmanoeuvre our rivals. It became a tool in my arsenal, one that set me apart from others in the organisation.

My dual life continued, with each day a test of my endurance and resolve. The final exams at university were looming, and I knew that passing them was crucial for my future. Meanwhile, my father's pressure to take on more responsibilities within the organization was intensifying. I was walking a tightrope, balancing my academic pursuits with the demands of the family business.

As the year drew to a close, the tension between my father and Don Carlo reached a boiling point. They both had clear visions for my future, and it was becoming increasingly difficult to reconcile their expectations. I knew that I needed to make a decision—one that would shape the rest of my life.

The final meeting was scheduled for tomorrow. It was the crucial moment when I had to showcase my plan and persuasively advocate for my selected course of action. I had spent countless hours preparing, analysing data, and crafting a strategy that I hoped would satisfy both my father and Don Carlo.

The night before the meeting, I couldn't find any rest. My mind was racing, filled with thoughts of the past year and the journey that had brought me to this point. I reflected on the challenges I had faced, the lessons I had learned, and the growth I had experienced. It had been a year of transformation, one that had tested my limits and shaped me into the person I am today.

I thought about the long nights spent studying, the crises at the port, and the delicate balance of power I had navigated. Each moment had contributed to my development, forging a path that was uniquely my own. I was no longer the boy who needed guidance at every step; I was a man capable of making his own decisions.

As dawn approached, I knew that the time had come to face my destiny. The final meeting would determine the course of my future, and I was ready to take control. I had a plan, a vision that combined the best of both worlds: my father's traditional values and Don Carlo's strategic foresight.

With a deep breath, I prepared myself for the day ahead. I knew that I had Don Carlo's support and my father's respect. It was time to step into my role fully, embracing the challenges and opportunities that lay ahead.

Now, you have heard the shortest summation of my entire life up to today, without omitting the most significant events I had in mind. That is how I became who I am today, and it has shaped me for the future that lies ahead. Now, I will get some hours of sleep before I have to attend the final meeting, which will decide my further path.

Goodbye's

It's a cold, stormy autumn evening as I emerge from the boxing arena. I needed to release some of my power and anger in order to maintain the calmness that everyone expected of me. Perhaps this was also the safest course of action. I can't guarantee anything, but once I experienced the thrill of blood and harm, I now frequently experience the familiar sensation from my first moments on earth, whether it's in a club or at the port.

The mansion felt more imposing than usual, its shadowed walls and intricate designs echoing the complexity of my thoughts. I entered the grand hall, where my father, Sandey, and Don Carlo awaited. Their contrasting personas filled the room with palpable tension. My father, with his stern yet caring demeanour, and Carlo, exuding an air of calculated power and authority, were already seated at the long mahogany table.

"Silas," Carlo began, his voice carrying the weight of unspoken expectations. "We have a lot to discuss tonight."

I took my seat, trying to calm the nerves that had been building up for days. This was it—the moment that would determine the direction of my future.

"Silas," my father echoed, his tone gentler but no less serious, "we've been talking, and there are some important decisions to be made about your future."

I nodded, knowing that my path would be heavily influenced by this conversation. Carlo leaned forward, his eyes piercing through the dim light. "You've done well, Silas. You've shown exceptional skill and dedication. That's why I believe you're ready to take on a more significant role within the family. By your eighteenth birthday, I want you to become the next Don."

My heart skipped a beat. The enormity of his words sank in slowly. To be the Don meant ultimate power and responsibility. It was both an honour and a burden.

"But," my father interjected, "I don't agree with that path for you, Silas. This life is dangerous. It's not what I want for my son. I want you to experience the real world, to start from the bottom, and to understand life outside this bubble."

Carlo's gaze hardened. "The 'real world' you speak of, Sandey, is filled with its own dangers, especially with the afterthought that everybody knows him in our circles. Silas is safer and more valuable here, with us. He has the potential to lead and expand our influence."

My father shook his head, determination etched on his face. "That may be true, but it's not about safety or influence. It's about Silas finding his own way. He needs to know what it's like to work a regular job and understand everyday people's struggles. That's how he'll become a real man."

I watched them argue, feeling the weight of their expectations press down on me. Both men cared deeply for me, but their visions for my future were worlds apart. The room grew silent as they awaited my response.

"I understand both of your perspectives," I began, choosing my words carefully. "Carlo, I appreciate your confidence in me and the opportunities you've provided. And Dad, I see the wisdom in your desire for me to experience life outside this world."

I took a deep breath, feeling the gravity of the moment. "But there must be a middle ground. What if I continue to study and work in the real world, as Dad suggests, while still maintaining my responsibilities here? I can learn from both worlds and decide my path based on that experience."

Carlo frowned, considering my proposal. My father's eyes softened slightly, hopeful.

"Silas," Carlo said slowly, "splitting your focus like that could be risky. The demands of this life are immense. You need to be fully committed."

"I understand the risks," I replied, "but I believe I can manage them." I want to be sure of my choices and to understand both sides before I commit fully to either."

My father nodded in agreement. "It's a reasonable compromise, Carlo. Let Silas prove himself in both worlds. He's young, and this experience will only make him stronger."

Carlo's eyes narrowed, his frustration evident. "Silas, you're underestimating the demands of this life. To lead this family, you need more than just a part-time commitment. You need to be immersed in it to understand every nuance and challenge, you must be immersed in it. The real world can wait. Our world **cannot**."

My father leaned forward, his expression resolute. "Silas, the real world offers experiences that you can't get here. It's about building character, understanding people, and seeing life from a different perspective. Those experiences will make you a better leader."

Carlo's voice grew more insistent. "Sandey, the real world is a distraction. Silas needs to be here, learning from me and preparing for the responsibilities he will inherit. The family needs a strong leader, not someone with divided loyalties, which you have been struggling with the entire time you've been here, haven't you?."

My father shook his head. "Carlo, strength comes from understanding all aspects of life. Silas will be a stronger leader if he has seen and experienced the struggles of ordinary people. It will give him empathy and wisdom, making him more grounded."

The tension in the room was palpable. Carlo's face hardened as he turned back to me. "Silas, if you leave now, even part-time, you're showing weakness to me. You're showing that you can't handle the pressure. This is not a job you can walk away from when it suits you. It's a lifetime commitment."

I met Carlo's intense gaze, feeling the weight of his words. "I understand, Carlo. But I believe that experiencing both worlds will make me a better leader. I need to know what it's like outside of this life. It's not about running away from my responsibilities; it's about understanding them from a different perspective."

Carlo shook his head, his frustration clear. "You're making a mistake, Silas. The family needs you here, fully committed. If you do anything less, you're jeopardizing everything we've accumulated over the years."

Images came into my mind as Carlo gave me the play gun, or the first real shot, and later the training and schooling he paid for so that we always found a middle way with my father's acceptance. However, there were other aspects that my father was unaware of, such as the studies I diligently worked on to complete a year ahead of schedule, and the absence of Sandey's guidance during our business trips and meetings. In the end, I would only get the high positions because of his guidance and teaching.

My father placed a hand on my shoulder. "Silas, you need to make your own choice. Whatever path you choose, I'll support you. But know this: true strength comes from knowing yourself and understanding the world around you completely."

The room fell silent as they awaited my decision. I took a deep breath, feeling the gravity of the moment pressing down on me. "I've made my choice," I said finally. Both of them looked at me, tensed and curious.

"I will continue my education and work in the real world, but I will also remain involved in the family business. I believe that balancing both will give me the insights I need to get before being able to become the best leader I can be." My words left my mouth before my brain had determined what they would mean for me.

Carlo's expression darkened, but he nodded reluctantly. "Very well, Silas. You've made your decision. But remember, the responsibilities of leadership are immense, and you must be ready when the time comes. I will give you until the age of twenty-fife, but you never know what will happen—any kind of early call out for you will result in a sudden stop and return." I nodded to him as I swallowed deeply, aware of the consequences of "a sudden stop".

My father smiled, a mixture of pride and concern in his eyes. "You're on the right path, Silas. This experience will shape you into the man you're meant to be."

I was determined to prove myself in both worlds, to become the leader they needed and the man I wanted to be.

I couldn't value or foresee it, but I knew they would test every part of me. Balancing the duality of my life, between the academic and the criminal, was a tightrope walk unlike any other. Each day presented new obstacles, forcing me to adapt and grow at a pace that felt overwhelming.

Preface

That was the way Silas started his young life under his harsh contracting guidance.

The next section of the book series will reveal what transpires during his years in the "real world" with regular jobs. If that even has a chance to end well, while he is still going to have to work for the mafia and continue his doctoral studies?

Additionally, other characters will appear. If you have read the "One Last..." series, you will find some of them familiar. However, what role will that complicated man play in our society? Will he become the next Don, or will he find another way of living for himself?

Have a wonderful day,

your L.H.K.

Like this the "A first…" series continues

A first **B**eat

A first **D**eath

A first **S**uffer-ring

A first **M**istake